The Ocean Was Salt

Loretta
Cobb

Livingston Press
University of West Alabama

Table of Contents

for my sweet Williams,
Cobb and Meredith

BEFORE WE CRAWLED TO TEARS

"The ocean was salt before we crawled to tears."

"The Wreck of the Thresher"—William Meredith

"Give it some gas, boy. Put the pedal to the metal!" My dad yelled this through a mist of Pabst Blue Ribbon as he popped his first one. He had pulled the grumbling Buick over to the side of the road so that I could take the wheel, get the feel of the car on the highway and then be the one to drive it down the smooth, slick beach. All around Daytona, cars cruise the Atlantic coast, their racing motors competing with the crashing tide for attention. I couldn't wait to make that drive.

Of course, I'd rather cruise with my buddies if I had any choice. I had driven their cars around our scrubby, inland town where nobody went faster than 30 miles an hour but us. This was my first legal drive though and the only present Big Papa was likely to give me for my fifteenth birthday. Mama had spent all day cooking my favorite food and decorating a creamy, chocolate cake that sagged in the middle.

The steering wheel felt loose, slippery, but I gunned the motor and hit the asphalt, tires screeching. The old car shook and jerked like my brother Bobby Gene having a seizure.

Mama wailed to her grandsons in the backseat, "Oh, God, he's gonna kill us all: your papa, Big Papa and us, too. Just because of Adam's learner's permit burning a hole in their pockets!" She patted the row of cotton tops as if she could now soothe away the fear she'd brought to the six frightened ice-blue eyes, glowing from the back seat in tiers, like three steps of terror. Turning them into deaf mutes, she had filled her emptiness with my brother's boys. Mama moaned toward the front, "Slow down, baby!"

Nobody else in my family seemed to realize children weren't deaf. Bobby Gene didn't seem to hear Mama either, just stared out at the flat farmland filled with citrus orchards. His eyes, glazed with grief, were dull, empty.

We never came to the beach overnight, but we'd drive down for the day, packed in like a can of salmon. When we reached New Smyrna, I drove right on the beach where the sand was smooth as glass, reflecting the colors of the sky right back at ol' Sol. It wasn't really any different from driving on the road, just slower, which made the car a little quieter.

I glanced at Mama in the rearview mirror, craning her neck to see the shoreline. She pushed salt and pepper curls away from her blue eyes, the same color as the water, and said, "Any time of day, it's just like a paintin', ain't it?" When Big Papa was in a good humor, we'd stay till sunset cause Mama loved to watch that mirror of a beach reflect the coppers and grays and pinks and blues all smudged together.

When I was little, I loved going down to Daytona with them more than anything in this world, but the older I got, the more embarrassed I was by the creaking ol' rattletrap of a car. It was a clear day, and the beach was already packed—a rainbow of sleek, shiny cars glinting at the sun in different shades of red and blue. I envied laughing couples, sweaty and oily, sprawled on orange and lime-green towels.

We drove several miles without finding a parking place, the tension escalating in the hot Buick. The kids squirmed and Big Papa fumed. Finally, he insisted on parking at an old motel and using their picnic area instead of the public beach. "It ain't near as crowded like 'at, Mama," he insisted, greasy brown hair blowing across his forehead. He plopped in a metal glider, faded mint green with rusty lattice. The sun-blanched stucco building with its flat roof and pale green shutters looked as if the owner didn't know the 1950s were over thirty years ago.

My brother Bobby Gene was still a kid himself, but he was raising three of his own. His rusty hairline receding, he already looked like an old man at 25. His kids sprang out of that ol' maroon Buick like puppies out of a pen, yelping and squealing as the brisk waves slapped 'em silly. I felt sorry for Bobby Gene, having to keep up with them all by himself, so I romped in the waves with 'em till they wore themselves down a little. It was pitiful the way they missed their mama. She worked at the hospital as an orderly until a few months ago when she moved in with an x-ray technician and started taking courses at the junior college. She told Bobby Gene, "I've outgrowed you."

Big Papa always drove with the windows down, his arm propped outside. When he shed his shirt, his left arm and his neck contrasted with the flabby, pale skin that covered the rest of him. He wore a white bikini bathin' suit anybody else would have thought was a joke, but he liked the way it bulged in the front. Oblivious to that pot of his he called a tool shed, he'd make vulgar bumps and grinds toward Mama just to make her soft cheeks turn rosy. She didn't wear makeup, didn't believe in it.

I was only 15 that summer, but I had figured out a few things. I figured intelligence was just a matter of how much ·

you were willing to read. I kept my nose stuck in a book, was right in the middle of one by D. H. Lawrence that Ms. Troncalli, my English teacher, recommended. She told me, "You're gonna love this one, Adam. Every morsel of food seems charged with sexual implications."

Ms. Troncalli was ugly as homemade sin but she could find a phallic symbol in a matchstick. The guys teased me about her, but I didn't care. She was fun to talk to, understanding, and she never tried to make a move on me or anything. She just read sex into all our assignments. I figured she was lonely.

In the middle of the day, the sweltering sun beat down on the smooth, gray ocean hotter 'n hell, but I liked it. It seemed just right to read *Lady Chatterly's Lover* with sweat dripping down my body. Mama sat at the cement table under a flapping umbrella with rusty spokes, which belonged to the Coronada Dunes Motel. She gazed at the water, a faraway, dreamy look in her eyes. I felt uncomfortable reading about fools plaiting flowers in their private parts with Mama close, but she didn't notice, didn't pay much attention to books. She didn't have any idea what I was up to. Besides, she was too busy keeping up with Bobby Gene's brood.

Other people seemed to have bought or rented an air of belonging that we could never assume no matter how hard Big Papa strutted and pretended. Wanting to appear a cool, detached loner, I spread my towel a little ways down the beach and kept moving it farther away, about an inch an hour. "I need to finish this for a book report next month," I lied to Big Papa, making sure he couldn't see the cover when he came snooping around.

"Hmnph. Looks like them fool school teachers could leave a boy alone in the summer time. You still got a week before you go back, ain't you? Shoot, if it was me, I'd be romping up and down this beach looking for some poontang. A boy your age . . . " His voice trailed off, lost in memories of his own youth as he waddled back up the path, stepping high and cursing the hot sand on his tender feet.

Like when I read *From Here to Eternity,* another well-worn book of Ms. T's, I was riveted. When an incredibly voluptuous woman in a red string bikini settled a few feet from me, I was astonished. She read, too, lying on a blue towel decorated with big, bright grapefruit. She never even looked at me, but I was in love. I had radar for eyes, could see her without looking. Every now and then she'd blink at the sun, shaking her thick black hair, and wipe the back of her neck. She mopped sweat from between her breasts, which were packed into that skimpy top like two juicy oranges about to bust out of those mesh bags at the roadside markets.

It was almost more than a boy could endure, reading steamy sex scenes while lying close to a woman in the sensual heat of sunny Florida. When I finished the book, I closed my eyes and listened to the lapping waves caress the shore.

I dozed into that realm where it's difficult to tell the difference between fantasy and reality until I heard the ugly cry of real life behind me. "Come and git it, boy!" Big Papa roared. "Soup's on. Heh heh." I covered my bulging green trunks with the faded yellow towel, trying to cover the frayed edge. I struggled with my bushy, curly hair but, without a comb, it was hopeless—like a mop of rusty coils stuck on my head.

I was careful not to get sand on the woman who had spread her towel so close to mine, but I sprinkled her moist, Copper-toned body in spite of myself. I gasped, "Oh, I'm sorry, m'am. Please excuse me." The scent of her suntan lotion hit my nostrils like a jolt of adrenaline.

She looked up with tranquil hazel eyes and said in a mellow voice, "What lovely manners! It's no problem, really. It's always good to see another book lover on the beach, especially one with good manners. What are you reading?"

Did she say book *lover*? Only that word buzzed in my head as I absorbed her words and again as I gasped for enough air to answer, "*Lady Chatterly's L-lover.*"

"Well," she smiled. "I'm impressed."

Should I say thank you? Should I just leave? Should I run like a scalded dog? "Me, too," I sputtered, adding, "see ya later."

I heard Big Papa pop another beer behind me, could sense his breathing down my neck. I didn't look up, not even when I saw a small black snake slithering across my path, as I made my way toward them. "I didn't even know there were snakes at the beach. Lookey yonder, y'all," I heard Big Papa exclaim.

"Well, Lord God," Mama said, spreading our picnic of ribs and slaw and chocolate and setting cold iced tea like only she could make on a cheap, plastic tablecloth. Her beaming smile faded, eyes pained as if she'd been slapped when she saw the sea gulls. As soon as she had the table all set up, the birds came swarming—upsetting the meal. "Look at that fat one, greedy as a Republican," she said, pointing to the one who gobbled all the crumbs she threw a few feet away, bullying the delicate sandpipers who trailed behind. Mama's feeble attempt to distract the creatures didn't deter them. The strutting, chattering birds wanted to lap grease from the grill where the sweet, succulent ribs had been hickory-smoked. We slapped the feathered vultures away like pesky flies and wolfed our food.

I said softly, "What a disappointment for a woman who cooked all day yesterday, but I tell you what, Mama. I can't blame the birds too much cause it was sure good eatin'."

Under the thin strand of hair he pulled across his balding scalp, Big Papa's face twisted in a sneer, as if it irked him I was sympathetic to Mama. His yellow teeth glistened in the sunlight, spittle bursting from his mouth as he started in about the woman's bikini. Of course, within earshot of the sunbather, he hollered, "Talk about good eatin'. . . . Whoooooeee!" He ogled the woman, then winked at me. "Mama, why don't you get you a red suit like 'at. Buddy was spending lots of time watching her today, wadn't he? You wouldn't have to lose more'n 50 pounds to get you a young boy all mooney-eyed over you."

Mama didn't say a word; she just kept eating ribs and never looked up, but I could see her pain, the way her plump shoulders drooped. I was just a teenager and I knew better. I helped her pack the chocolate-smeared dishes in the picnic basket, while Big Papa chased the kids as close to the red bathing suit as possible, hollering, "Whoooooeee!" over and over. He cocked his head toward me the first few times, but I ignored him.

Then he slanted his eyes toward the woman for encouragement, but she ignored him. Finally she scowled at him, an awful thing overtaking that tranquil, smooth face, which twisted and wrinkled like a rubber mask into scorn. That stopped him. His mouth gaped in disbelief, his eyes exploded.

Not to be outdone, he did a sleazy bump and grind right in her face, but she was composed again. Unflappable.

"Come on, younguns, let's go find us a friendly place to play," Big Papa said, yanking the youngest one too hard.

"Help, Papa," the cotton-top wailed toward Bobby Gene who ambled self-consciously toward them.

"Don't worry, son. He ain't got but two more beers," Mama told me, flapping the crumbs at the greedy birds. It wasn't near sundown, but she was ready to go, her face creased with despair. The kids slept all over me and Mama in the back seat while Big Papa snored and Bobby Gene drove that rattly Buick like a bat outta hell through the scrubby, sandy wilderness all the way home. For miles, Mama watched the sunset over rows of green soybeans and peanuts. Crimson swirls and smoky grey clouds peeped through the dark lace of pecan trees along the horizon.

AND THE WORD WAS GOD

Sometimes I feel like I've outlived my life. I've always been claustrophobic, can't stand to be locked in some smothering tee-niney place. My asthma would act up so bad if I was locked in a closet I'd die before morning. I ain't ever been on an airplane and I'm proud of it, but I know how it would feel. What I'm going through is worse than any airplane, but kinda like it. It's like my head's got clouds in it and my mind is locked in the closet, can't get out for air. I can't let it out much because when I do it acts up, says the wrong words, gets things mixed up.

At first, I don't know whether their voices are imaginary or real. Since the intercom was on, they started out whispering after I'd had time to go to sleep, but their voices got louder. I knew when Ladonna bit her lip, could see it as clear as if I were in the room.

"But you'd feel better if you took anti-depressants, Daddy. You have an impossible load as primary caregiver."

"I ain't gonna let it get ME down," Louie said, not listening, but figuring out what to say next. Course I could see what he meant: *That Wellbutrin she's taking don't seem to make her butt well.*

"If you'd go to a support group you'd see how much this drains you," my daughter pleaded.

"I don't need no support and your mama can't stay by herself," Louie said with a ring of finality. Case closed. But of course, Ladonna's shrill voice ain't gonna leave it alone.

"Jeanne Ruth said she'd come stay with her while we go. You need to get out. Mama needs a different caregiver sometimes." She clears her throat and goes on, "You can be so negative, so pessimistic. Mama doesn't need to hear how bad she feels drummed in her head."

"Listen, girl, you're not here day in and day out. When I say she ain't able to do whatever you want her to do, I know what I'm talking about," Louie snarls. "She wasn't able to go for a ride today. Period."

"You know what you're talking about, alright. Just like you know more than the dietician," Ladonna snaps back.

"I been feedin' Mama for 15 years on that diet. I know what makes her sugar go up. I can keep it down," his drill sergeant's voice replies.

"Oh give me a break. So you know more than the experts. You are so damn stubborn," Ladonna shrieks.

"This is my business, by God," Louie shouts. "She's my wife and I love her more than life itself!" He's worked up now. Everything is real quiet for a little while. Then he starts in again, "You the one thinks you know everything. You thought that physical therapist was gonna take a load off me, told me to take a nap while she's here. I have to stay up here so I can answer questions for Mama."

"No you don't," Ladonna wails. "Quit controlling. You don't think anybody can do anything but you, and Mama needs somebody cheerful at least some of the time. All you do is watch sports. I'm worried about your health; your devotion could kill you. You both need a break from each other."

"You don't know how bad off she is," Louie says defensively. "She's losing her mind."

That's when I start coming out of that bed.

Ladonna goes on though, "I know. She called today and left a message on my machine that turned into a prayer. She told God I've been stealing her panties. That's why I want you to talk to this social worker. She can help us work together."

I slam my bedroom door, grip the cane so hard my hands will be sore tomorrow, and march down the hall. Their mouths look like Casper's and another friendly ghost's, saying Oooo. "Y'all talking about me!" I say, my voice blazing.

"No, Mama," Louie whispers.

"Yes, Mama," Ladonna says at the same time. "We've been talking about our family, about all of us, but not like talking *about* you." Her voice soothing, musical, she hugs me toward her softness.

My complaint is lucid, "Louie, you need to congratulate me, not criticize me. Don't say I'm losing my mind."

"Darling, why would I criticize you?" he says, his pale eyes innocent as a boy's. "I love you more than anything. You know that." He's got that expression that means he thinks I'm a baby. He shakes his head and rubs the stubble of his G. I. hair cut.

Ladonna pounces, "What logic! Of course, you love her, but it doesn't follow that you won't criticize, Daddy."

For once he's quiet. I think he heard her. Then he turns to me, the hurt in those blue eyes cutting into me more than his criticism. "Mama, you know I try as hard as I can. I do for you all day long, every day." I think of the time he put his head in his hands at the kitchen table and boohooed; my own eyes sting. Before we saw any of the doctors, when it first became more trouble to Louie than help, for me to pitch in with the cooking.

"Sit down, Mama. We'll all talk," Ladonna whispers.

"I know I can be ornery." I feel for the elevated recliner behind me. "Tell you the truth it's so much trouble to get up and down I should just go back to bed."

"That's right," Louie jumps on the chance for confirmation. "You ain't able to sit up."

Ladonna screams, "Daddy, stop saying that. She is obviously *ABLE*. Look, she's sitting right there, proving you wrong!"

I sit up straight, try to look able, but I'm tired and I know it's too late to be thinking. We all talk a few minutes and then Ladonna helps me back to bed. I hear them murmur, then the door shuts softly as I drift to sleep again. Occasionally I jerk awake when some sportscaster screeches like it's the second coming.

When Ladonna first started this business with new doctors, I tried to put my foot down. My daughter bribed me by taking me out to eat Chinese food when we went into town to see doctors at the medical center.

I will give that eye doctor this: she let me take that vision test over, the one where you shoot at flashing lights for half an hour. I knew that machine was broken, but they didn't believe me. I asked my eye doctor, "Do *YOU* think I need to see a psychiatrist?"

The doctor just looked confused. Naturally she's a colored woman, since my daughter, the professor, picked her out. She stiffened, raised her nose a little and said in that Boston brogue, "I know hardly anything about psychology. I specialized in detached retinas."

Well, detach my retina, I thought to myself in a voice like Polly Holiday's when she used to tell Mel to kiss her grits. Polly was a local girl who became as famous as Gomer Pyle.

Ladonna doesn't cry in front of me, but I see her puffy eyes when she comes over to watch *The Wheel* every night. I've long since given up enjoying the show. Now, I enjoy interrupting the game her and Louie play, trying to beat each other to the clue. I used to play, too, but now I can't concentrate long enough to get a word, let alone a phrase or one of those before-and-after clues.

I just watch Vanna model them pretty clothes and admire her hairdo. She's got several babies, now. Me and her been through a lot together. Sometimes I feel closer to Vanna than to my own daughter. Now *Vanna* dresses *right*! "Reckon it's gonna rain tomorrow?" I ask the Wheel champions.

"Wait just a minute, Mama," Louie growls.

I mutter, "I ain't your mama."

Once they guess *in the palm of my hand,* I interrupt again. "Now when is it y'all goin' to It'ly, Ladonna?"

"Not for a long time yet, Mama," she patronizes, "it's ten days from now."

"Umm hmm," I respond. As soon as the boy from Chicago gets mobbed by the winner's family squeezing into the red convertible they've won, Louie switches the remote control to *Nightly News.*

"You know they're having a war? Ain't Yugoslavia close to It'ly?" I ask her.

"Not really," Ladonna says, suddenly busy filling up the foot spa.

Louie joins in, like he knows all about it since he fought in China 50 years ago. "Kosovo ain't nowhere near Rome, Mama."

I tell 'em, "I ain't lost a thang over there myself."

Ladonna's a sweet girl, but I wish she'd fix herself up. All them professors at the college look like they're in a hobo contest, wearing them blue jeans and big old tennis shoes with skirts. Right now, that crumpled denim blouse hangs out of her skirt. I say, "Hon, you want to use my iron sometimes?"

"No, thanks, Mama," Ladonna snaps, her cleavage wrinkling as she bends down with my foot spa steaming. When we finish, she rubs my legs with a soft, fluffy towel.

She smiles while she massages my feet with peppermint lotion and instructs me, "They say this improves circulation, so maybe it will get more blood to your brain." She also brings me ghinko and puts rosemary oil in my shampoo to help my memory.

Louie don't make fun of her to her face. He hates seeing them eyes of hers puffy, too.

Smelling like peppermint, I crawled in the new hospital bed. I tried not to remember the pretty carved headboard they sold when they moved this contraption in my bedroom, but focus on Ladonna's pallet and her willingness to stay overnight and do whatever it takes. I had to pee all night because of them water pills, but she never got up to help me. It wasn't like her to just lie there mummified while I struggled all the way down to the end of the bed where the rails gapped.

I knew what was wrong, but I couldn't make the words

come. Instead of a bed with collapsible rails for folks who can still get up and down alone, they'd brought me a bed rail for folks mostly bedridden. Holding on to both sides of what felt like burglar bars, I had to inch myself down all the way to the foot of the mattress and then crawl through the place where the nurses pull you out of bed and make you walk.

Toward dawn Ladonna muttered, "Mama, if you'll quit grumbling and just try to get used to having a hospital bed, I'll call the medical equipment place as soon as they open."

When they brought new rails and apologized for blundering, Ladonna burst into tears. "Oh my God, Mama, I wouldn't have let you struggle, but I figured you *had* to learn to use your new bed. I hated lying there, making you do it on your own. I don't ever know what to do any more. Damn!" She bit her lip, the bright red blood as startling as that dark blood years ago when she first had a menstrual period. I held her close to my breast as long as either one of us could stand it.

"My baby's been so good to me," I whisper in her ear. Her nails dig into my back, but I don't let on.

The next day, we went to see this little foreign neurologist, Dr. Bislami. He patted me on the shoulder, asked me if I knew what day it was, his hand shaky. He looked as old as I felt. When I asked him if he thought I needed to see a psychiatrist, he handed me free samples of Zoloft and answered, "No. We can take care of you right here."

Do you think Ladonna was grateful? No. She pitched a fit: "How dare you give her antidepressants without asking any more questions! You ruled out Parkinson's; that's all we need from you. We will not be back!" She grabbed our purses, blood veins in her neck popping out fit to bust. I looked from one to the other, embarrassed.

"American women!" the doctor shrugged, his dainty mouth twisted in a smirk. "You can drag your mother to different doctors if you like, but the truth remains—she is simply 81 years old. In pretty good health at 81 I'd say."

Hobbling down the hall, I gushed, "Dr. Bislami's skin looked even darker when he smiled showing those white teeth."

Ladonna shivered, "There was something mean about his smile. That old-country arrogance drives me to murderous fantasies."

Sunday afternoons, I went to Baskin-Robbins with my great grandchildren. Louie said I couldn't have no sugar-free ice cream cause it might run my sugar up. (Ever since I've had sugar diabetes, he's been bossing me around.) He said I ought to bring the ice cream home and put it in the freezer till we check my sugar.

When I tried to tell Jeanne Ruth, my granddaughter, what I wanted, it came out wrong. "Get me two scoops and Louie one," I grinned. She twinkled with understanding. We've been in a few minor rebellions in our time, me and her.

Then she said, those velvety brown eyes straining to get it right, "Did you want a cone or a cup?"

"Just get me and him both a cup," I said.

"But you want a two-scoop cup, right?" she smiled patiently. Then I heard myself answering, "Naw just get me a cone and him a cup. We don't really need but one scoop." That cone was enough indulgence. It hurt my brain to cheat on Louie now, confused me.

The baby licked Ladonna's chocolate cone, getting it all over her little pink sun dress and Ladonna's red linen mini skirt. The creamy brown streaks on Ladonna's blouse dwindled to watery. I wanted to laugh because she was dressed up in a way that didn't look a bit like a grandmother ought to. Probably to go out somewhere with that young boy she's been seeing. "Honey, that skirt's awful wrinkled," I told her. Her round, prissy face turned scarlet as that skirt.

Before the blazing sun melted it, I swirled my tongue around the cold ridges of melting "ocean bubble-gum" flavor on the cone Jeanne Ruth handed me. I picked out a green gummy fish that slid between my breasts. Like to tickled those littl'uns to death. Buddy squealed so loud I thought he'd pop an eardrum. I usually ordered the same flavor they did and just told Louie it was sugar-free. I ate my ice cream, ignoring the mess. I wasn't going anywhere but to bed. I didn't mind that blue sweetness on my blouse.

"Meemaw, didn't Papaw tell you to save yours till later?" Jeanne Ruth asks, the smile replaced by concern.

I hate to worry her, but I ain't gonna save this blame ice cream till later neither. That's why I was trying to get two scoops—one to save. Jeanne Ruth lets it pass. Then when I try to give her some money to pay for everybody's treat, she won't take it. "Wait a minute!" I yell. "We need to go back to that bank and get my money. I know I had more than this when we started out. I musta counted them one dollar bills 20 times." Then I mumble to myself, "But they wouldn't have no ice cream at the bank."

I know it's not coming out right before I see those brown ambers look in the back seat at my daughter's knowing eyes, emerald as a cat's. Their eyes lock in a moment of understanding as if I'm blind because I can't say the words right. But there's love and pain in their glance, too, and it breaks my heart. There ain't nothing we can do, and we all know it.

That little psychiatrist's blond ponytail shook so much I thought he'd whinny any minute. Behind tiny steel-rimmed glasses, his baby blue eyes went cloudy and goofy when I asked him point blank, "What is vascular dementia?"

"Nothing much," he said, "just that you'll have a lower IQ."

"See?" I glared triumphantly at my daughter. I told you I didn't need no psychiatrist!"

Of course, Ladonna challenged him, "I didn't think we used that terminology now," she started before he cut her off.

"I use it to keep things simple," he told her.

"Humph," she said when he stood up and tapped my folder on his desk. As soon as we reach the elevator, Ladonna wilts. She's only in her 50's, but my baby's tired already with dark circles under her eyes like a bull's eye.

"The Geriatric Psychiatric wing is impressive, don't you think?" She likes saying *geriatric psychiatric* as often as she can. My daughter overrates rhyme.

I touch her soft hand, its aging spots still a marvel to me, "Baby, you worry too much, think you can fix everything."

She frowns at me, then wheels that little Japanese Toyota out of the parking lot and across the street too fast, leaving sparks and squeals behind. Then she zooms into the drive-thru lane like a bat outta hell. She speaks to the fast-food squawk box as if it's human, "I want one of those six packs. . . . " She fumbles for the right word just like I do these days, the wrinkled forehead grappling with the dictionary in her brain. Her gray blonde curls shake fiercely when the speaker answers, "Say whaaaaat? Drive up to the window, baby."

"You know those six-for-six-dollars roast beef sandwiches?" Ladonna squints into the voice's amazed face, on the other side of the glass window. "Don't y'all call that a six pack? I could use a beer but I know you don't sell that kind of six-pack. . . ."

Then the dark face is all teeth, the heavy bosom jiggling with laugher. "Girlfriend, you think you at Arby's? This is McDonald's! You got to go down one more drive."

Some women would die of embarrassment, but Ladonna lets out a lusty laugh and beats the steering wheel she's so tickled. My baby laughs so hard she cries. She dabs at her streaming eyes with a wadded up Kleenex she ought not to be re-using.

"Look who's lost her memory now," I quip.

My daughter winks at me. She's quick. "I guess I'm the one who needs geriatric psychiatric help, huh?" I try not to notice she's found another chance to say those blooming words. We're both tired, quiet. I lapse into that void where I'm not sure where we are. Passing landmarks like that spaghetti loop at the interstate helps, but some of the time we might as well be in Timbuktu. I can feel the heat steaming from the sugary sand, imagine a vapor of steam rising from it. The ocean stretches for miles along here without a sign of human life. I like this stretch, the way we always fall silent, don't need any words for a while. I strain to stay focused, concentrate on the sapphire line at the edge of the ocean, the splotches of emerald and turquoise that lead out to it. I know that's where God lives, right inside the line that looks like it's been drawn by a fountain pen using indigo ink. I used to love that song *Mood Indigo* when folks danced all night at The Club Rose. I didn't know a thing yet about blues that go right down to your toes.

We love my local doctor (Ladonna loves him a little too much, I think), but even he gives up on me. I can see it in those soft eyes that glimpse my chart, then look straight into my eyes and feign cheer, "How are you today, Miz Essie?"

I tell him I'm fine and then Ladonna takes over: "I wish you'd tell her to quit wearing panties with nobody there but us."

The doctor's face colors as he writes in my chart right quick, so she turns to me, "We've seen it, Mama, and you're gonna fall trying to get 'em down fast enough. Hell, I don't wear 'em myself."

"I know," I tell that hussy pointedly. The doctor writes faster and gets out of that tiny room in a hurry.

Louie and Ladonna felt like giving up on me, but they never did. She was on the phone to some adult day care one day, which made my stomach cramp so I headed to the potty. Ladonna hung up in mid-sentence, yelling, "Help her with those damn panties!"

It was done too late. She nearly wore a hole in the carpet when she scrubbed in the hall. She told me when I tried to help, "I've got just enough sense to know this could be me any day now; I'm not offended. You don't need to stoop down here."

Ladonna tries to turn the accident into an adventure, filling the foot spa with soothing warm water and vibration, to wash my legs and feet. I wash off from the waist up at the sink.

When she leaves, Ladonna tells us in a trembling voice, "I had an e-mail today suggesting we pay more attention to the courage of 80-year-old Americans, learn from them. I'm so proud you were a Marine, Daddy, gave that anti-Semitic maniac hell."

Louie's face brightened, "Thank you. We been through it. Born during war time. Come out of the Depression straight into another war. Yeah, real depression, not the Zoloft kind huh?"

He enfolds Ladonna, rubbing his bristly unshaved chin against her scalp like he used to when she was a baby. She tunes up but gets a-hold of herself, "It sure as hell gave you courage, both of you, and I love you for it."

"Bye, we appreciate everything," Louie says and turns those wet blue eyes toward me, but my mind's already gone to worrying about my share of the money on Mama's flowers for the coffin blanket.

I break the dam that makes his tears gush when I ask, "When's the funer—"

"Come on, baby, let's get you back to bed." He wipes his eyes with his sleeve. Then he laughs, "I remember when it wasn't near as hard to get you in the bed." I can feel the smile begin to wrap around my face.

I'm not even tellin' the worst things, don't want to remember them myself. The confusion: I swore I saw Ladonna climb up a ladder and in my window to steal my panties, but the window is so low she wouldn't need a ladder. She promised she had not hidden them nor stolen them, told me lots of folks with dementia hoard things. I hated not knowing whether to believe her. The fears: guns, dogs, orgies where I can't tell Louie and them nurses and sitters from the CMT blur.

The bottom line: when I hear that sitter, cigarette-raspy, call Ladonna to say she can't lift me by herself no more, I know it clear and cold. Right then, I can see it's over.

Godamighty, I've loved Louie these last weeks like I hadn't in years. I hate to leave that boy, them blue eyes still shining when he pulls me up to the potty like we was gonna do the tango. But he can't be wakin' up through the night and keep going, and neither can my daughter. It takes a young, strong man to lift a big-boned woman.

That sitter jerked my arm last night and then swore she didn't. Louie's face creased like he couldn't stand not knowing who to believe. I didn't either, so I said, "Maybe I dreamed it."

God knows I tried to use that bedpan, but my kidneys refused. Depends broke me out in them old whelps fierce as a fire ant. The idea of one of them catheters and a feedin' tube so somebody could rip off Medicaid ain't a pretty picture. Main thing wrong with that picture is me in it. I gave it all the concentration I could hold on to when I told God, "O.K., friend, we done run this out. I'm ready."

It wasn't 24 hours before that ambulance came swinging low to take me by the hospital on my way Home. I held on in my bedroom till Ladonna come runnin' in, out of breath—ready to face the Prince of Darkness if she had to. She figured it out quick though; she knew I was ready. In the emergency room, she filed my nails, then painted them during the night propped up in the bed with me in spite of those hoses they had in my nose for that useless oxygen. I was so tired, but I worked my droopy lungs hard as I could till my first-born grandson came. Once I knew he was on his way, me and God both backtracked, held on with all our might. I knew my grandson was in the hospital before anybody else knew, felt his presence come over me ten minutes before I felt the warmth, the strength, of that forty-year-old hand smelling like dirt and roses. At last, I closed my eyes and smiled, released.

I howled when Ladonna made the undertaker bury me in those black step-ins even though it wasn't customary. I hovered just long enough at the gravesite to see that my body was wearing those lacy panties. Then I floated out toward the endless blue peace, that wordless line between the sea and sky.

THAT FALL

We stretched out on our backs to find the Milky Way, sharing the sticky caramel and chocolate named for it almost every night that fall. I never understood what that mysterious galaxy had to do with an ordinary candy bar. In those days, even with the steel mills in town, the stars were so clear and bright it took my breath away: the whole sky lit up with diamonds, rubies, and aquamarines. My sister and I watched the stars almost every night that fall with Buster, our neighbor—even after we had to bring extra quilts for cover. Sometimes he wrestled Lucinda under their own quilt, but I was absorbed in the stars, trying to see Saturn's ring or Venus or Mars.

"Hey, Bonita, show us Uranus," Buster teased, sending my sister into giggles. Ignoring Buster's stupid jokes, I continued to instruct them even though he was 13 and she pretended to be, but I was only nine. They were content to lie on their backs and star gaze, but I showed them how to find Orion, Cassiopeia, and the Bear. For my first independent assignment in third-grade science class I ordered a set of booklets on the solar system. The smooth, slick pamphlets fit into a red box, which looked just like a book on the shelf. It was the first time I had bought something to read besides comic books.

Buster shivered, rubbing his arms to keep warm. "It's too cold for quilts on the ground tonight, let's flatten those old boxes and put them under the covers like air mattresses." During the summer, we had spent hours on cardboard boxes sliding down the sloping bank of shaggy, emerald grass in the side yard. Summer seemed long ago on this frosty October night.

Lucinda looked up at him under long lashes, pleading, "First, let's have one last ride in them. We can take turns, ok?" She touched his arm lightly.

"Sure," Buster said, his eyes getting that swimmy look when she touched him—the look that made him say Lucinda was old for her age. "I'm first," he announced.

We got a running start and pushed him down the hill, squealing with the exhilaration of danger. It was thrilling to take a chance on breaking our necks. We stayed out as late as we wanted since Mama worked nights. When Suzie, our live-in sitter from the Baptist college, came in shivering in her satin cheerleader outfit around seven, she said we could stay out longer because Rhett, our stepfather, needed to sleep before his shift at 11.

Finally, though, it was so cold and dark outside even Buster had to go home. Lucinda glared at me accusingly when she couldn't open the front door. She rattled it so hard I thought the window panes might fall out.

"I know I left the door unlocked," I snapped.

"Go see if the back door is unlocked," she ordered.

I took my time to spite her, enjoying the puffs of vapor as if I were smoking. I tried to open the bathroom window from the back porch, but it, too, was locked. I rapped hard against the window panes, but there was no answer. When the streetcar passed, its orange sparks flying from the overhead cables reminded me of the night my father said he heard Santa on the rooftop. I shivered, from the cold as well as the memory of my daddy's gentle reassurance when I feared the sparks from the chimney might burn Santa. Sometimes I missed my dad. I wondered if he could get Rhett or Suzie to come to the door. Uneasy, I raced back to the front porch with the bad news, telling my sister I had knocked my knuckles raw on the windowpanes.

"Hey, that's an idea," Lucinda said. "Let's look in all the windows until we figure out where they are. Then we can make them hear us." Her nose was red from the cold, like Rudolph.

We could see the blond coffee table in front of the sofa, the whatnots in the corner and the scratchy old 78 rpm record going round and round. We heard music coming from the old mahogany record player, but nobody was there. "Listen," I whispered, my hand at my ear, "is it *Sunset Serenade* or *Canadian Sunrise*?"

"Who cares?" Lucinda snarled. She stalked away. I felt a sense of dread as I followed behind her, wondering if she was mad at me or at Suzie for locking us out. She pulled the concrete blocks stacked near the barbecue pit up to the bedroom window so we could climb up. "The blinds are down, but if we try hard, we can see through the cracks of light at the edge," Lucinda said, pointing to the small shaft of hazy, golden light. "They've got to be in the house or we'd have heard them going out."

Making it a game, like the Bobbsey twins solving a mystery, I suggested, "If Rhett's still asleep, maybe we can wake him up." However, my sister's forehead creased with worry as she strained to see inside. Then her mouth opened like she was going to vomit, and her eyes opened even wider. "Let me see," I whispered, somehow feeling shame already. My big sister didn't even seem to hear me. Looking through the crack of soft light, I saw my stepfather holding Suzie down. He pressed his hands down around her shoulders, and she cried out, her eyes closed and her mouth open, screaming.

"Is he gonna kill her?" I asked, terrified.

Lucinda's voice was flat, world-weary at twelve, when she answered, "I don't think so."

Only then did I realize Rhett and Suzie were both undressed, her large breasts jiggling. Her dark nipples looked hard and puckered like Mama's when she was in the tub. It was the first time I had ever seen Rhett's butt. Suddenly I felt guilty for seeing them.

"Come on, we'll sit in the basement out of the wind," Lucinda said, buttoning my coat at the top.

"It's dark in there," I protested, "and scary." I hated the musty smell, the dank darkness of it. I had wanted to build a playhouse there for my tea sets, but it was too dreary and the mold stung my eyes.

"Ain't no darker than what's inside," Lucinda said, her lips pouting, her eyes working hard not to cry. "Besides, there's no wind blowing down there."

We sat under the house, huddled in the dark for a long time. Mother's favorite rug, the one with roses, had mildewed, its sour smell filling the air. Lucinda decided to tell me ghost stories to pass the time. I didn't think it was a good choice, but I didn't say so. Something inside me had frozen like the icicles I had seen along the roof that morning.

Lucinda smirked more than usual on the way to school the next day. When I couldn't stand it any longer, I asked her, "How come you look like you just treed Jesus?"

"Well, Goody Two Shoes has learned to be sacrilegious!" she jeered. Then she boasted, "I woke Mama up and told her about last night!"

I was tired before the day even started. After that, Mama,

Rhett and Suzie had long conversations behind closed doors. When Suzie moved her things out and went back to live on campus, I hated seeing the satin cheerleader outfits go. Her soft, dark curls bounced above her pinched face as she made a dozen trips to a car whose driver never came inside. Several weeks later, Suzie—in a state of repentance—sent a letter to all of us.

October 17, 1952

Dear Mrs. Pearl and Mr. Rhett,

I just want to tell you all how much I miss you and that I am praying for you every day. I am sorry for any hurt I caused your family. I will always love Lucinda and Bonita like "little sisters."

Me, I'm fine but I still hate going to classes. Ha Ha! I know I was terrible about my school work while I was back-slid, but I have found the Lord again, and He blesses my every hour. (Except in class. Ha Ha! My math teacher is mean as ever, and boy is it hard when I really do try.)

Mainly, I wanted to tell you that a famous evangelist/healer will be on our campus next week. Brother Billy Martin will be here on Saturday when I have to cheer at a game out of town, but I hope all of you can come to hear him. My parents say he can heal hurt as well as the halt and the lame. I hate to miss him, but I'm so close to Jesus right now that I know my sins are cleansed and if He called right now I'd be ready to go home to the Lord.

Yours in Christ,

Suzie

XXX OOO,

Rhett and I both got teary when we read the letter, but Mom lit a cigarette and stamped out of the room, her high heels clomping louder than usual. Lucinda seemed untouched in any way by the letter, but she did follow Mama down the hall. "I thought that was a sweet letter," I told Rhett.

"Yeah, baby, I think it was, too," he croaked hoarsely.

Mama said Rhett was desperate for some kind of quick solution. He was more fidgety and irritable than when he first quit drinking. Lucinda and I ate dinner quickly, then dressed to go to a Saturday afternoon movie, eager to escape the tension.

I heard Rhett and Mama talk while they finished the liver and onions she'd fixed. "This will give you strength, Rhett, pick you up some, maybe even settle that temper down," Mama said. I looked back to see her sopping a biscuit in the thick, brown gravy, her diamond ring making rainbows. Her solution to almost any problem was to build up your iron by eating liver.

He whined, "Seems like giving up the bottle could keep a feller out of trouble."

"Or at least out of other people's britches." Mama scraped the plates hard enough to scratch off the gold trim around the troubadour singing to a fair maiden on the platter. "I ain't sure there is a cure for that."

"I gotta find some peace of mind, baby—"

"I hope it's peace of *mind* you're looking for," she barked. As their squabble escalated, I sneaked another look through my open door. Her back toward him now, he gazed at her soft, pale shoulders, then her shapely legs.

"Pearl, Pearl, the girl with pearlized skin," he muttered almost to himself, then said louder, "you're such a beautiful woman, all any man could want. I don't know how I could have been such a fool." Her back toward him registered no response. He fingered the grapes on the oilcloth during the silence, finally pronouncing, "I'm going to hear Billy Martin whether you come or not."

"La de dah," she snorted.

"The Bible says a woman should follow her husband where he leadeth—" Rhett began.

She cut him off, "Yeah, well my mama taught me a passage like that only applies if you get yourself an A-#1, good husband. Besides, Phil used to say religion is the last refuge of a scoundrel, and I'm beginning to think he had a double-strength point."

"I wouldn't quote my ex if he was such an S. O. B.," Rhett mumbled as I headed down the hall and off to the escape of make-believe at the College Theater, our local picture show.

We didn't hear any more about the letter, but the next Saturday, we were scrubbed so clean I was surprised I still had skin. Mama dressed us to a fare-thee-well, drug out our red suits with tabs on the jackets and pleated skirts. Lucinda pouted all afternoon because she had to dress like her baby sister, but it didn't do any good. Agitated, Mama must have tried on ten outfits, finally settling on a soft, baby blue wool dress. She looked beautiful, even wore some blue eye shadow.

Rhett did his share of primping, too. His hair was so slick by the time he got it like he wanted it I could have fried okra in it. He had grown a mustache, which Mama hated.

"Still trying to look like Clark Gable to keep up with that nickname?" Mama called to him from the bedroom. "I need to use that mirror, too." He splashed some Old Spice on his face and went toward his sweater drawer. "What did I do for encouragement before I met you, Pearl?"

"Let me guess," she chided.

I didn't like Brother Billy Martin from the moment we saw him positioned at the entranceway to his tent. The man and the tent both seemed like they'd be more at home in the circus than on a college campus. The khaki tent was scalloped like my Easter dress, the "doors" flapping in the evening breeze. Music spilled out from the center of the tent where a group of singers clapped and sang "Gimme that old time religion, gimme that . . ." Even though the tent was huge, I felt claustrophobic before I ever entered it. I worried that, with her asthma, Mama might suffocate in there.

Brother Martin welcomed people with the widest smile I had ever seen. Long before I understood the words, I knew about hypocrisy and the predatory preacher's ego. He strutted toward a woman in front of us and asked her in an amplified voice, "How many souls have you brought to Christ today, Sister Murphy?"

I glanced back up the hill where we parked the car to see if folks there had heard the man. The heavyset, pale woman answered in a timid, high-pitched voice that didn't go with her body, "A few."

The preacher slapped her hard on the back and said, "Gung Ho all the way. Keep it up, sister," then boasted louder, "We had 157 come down front in Tulsa last night. Praise Jeeheesus!"

That time, folks on the hill did look down to see what the racket was. The crimson and golden leaves scattered down the hillside, reflecting the last light of day where the sun streaked the sky with paler shades of the same colors. A patch of intensely bright yellow ginkgo leaves on the ridge glowed as if spotlit. Suzie had said the students called this area the amphitheater because they had informal concerts in the small valley that faced the hilltop as if it were a stage. They also came there to "make out."

Brother Martin's eyes feasted on Lucinda, scanning her small breasts as if she were naked. He swooped down, leaned closer, and hugged her close enough to feel her breasts, "Welcome to the House of the Lord, child," he whispered too close to her ear. He hugged all young girls with breasts too tight, but he skipped me entirely. I glared at him. After Lucinda's padded bra got mashed in, pushing the tips of the pointed cones inward, she glared, too.

This famous evangelist looked ordinary as polished deceit to me: slick, curly hair the color of rust, huge hands, a thick, football player's body, and a toothy smile. I enjoyed hearing the choir of pretty girls from the stage, but as soon as the local preachers competed in their introductory testimonials, I gave in to the sleepiness that had threatened me for half an hour and dozed with my head on Mama's shoulder. I jerked awake, startled by a thundering voice, flapping canvas and the metallic screech of rusty pulleys. The center of the tent's top opened dramatically, only the pole and the red, white and blue of the American and Christian flags visible on the tower-like structure that topped the tent. The pole shook slightly but our attention was diverted by Brother Billy who pranced around the stage. Breathing hard, he oozed a hypnotic sensuality, a sanctimonious sleaze spilling out—higher, louder, "He's a-coming back, brothers and sisters, and you'd better be ready."

He paused, signaled men stationed by the pulleys at the tent's edge who rolled the tent's ceiling open, and hundreds of balloons—red, white and blue—rose into the darkness, the flags barely visible as we watched the balloons soar above them. The evangelist soothed smugly, "On the day of Judgement, friends, you, too, can float peacefully up to your Savior free of the burden of sin. Just like these balloons, light as a feather!"

The display was so stunning, I believed for a moment that the hilltop was Heaven. Maybe the glowing ginkgo had been a sign. Once the tent top was open, the crisp air rushed in, drawing my attention to the bright, clear stars above us. I tried to imagine being weightless, balloon-like, as a way to ignore Brother Billy who repeated the same message over and over.

The preacher's performance continued. "You never know when the Judgment will come, and we better be ready to fly away." The girls' choir sang "I'll Fly Away." The minister slapped his Bible in rhythm with them, unable to give up the spotlight for a second. Brother Billy jerked his tie, shed his jacket and continued. "It could be tomorrow. It could be right now!"

His voice, now hoarse, strained to be heard over the booming of what sounded like a cannon. Then I saw the fireworks explode in the sky: red, white and blue. The men around the edge of the tent cranked ropes as the side walls rolled up to provide a better view of the extravaganza from the hilltop. Sparks fell around us, too close. One of the men rolling the canvas wall back down yelped when a red spark landed on his shirt.

"Don't that smell remind us of hell fire!" Brother Billy shouted, grinning. "And don't worry, this tent is fireproof, just as fireproof as your soul can be if you'll get right with the Lord tonight. Brothers and sisters, I saw that molten steel when I was crossing the viaduct coming into your beautiful magic city from the airport today. Right then, I said to myself, 'Brother Billy, that's how it's gonna be in hell fire! Yeah, that's how it's gonna be, like swimming in a flaming river.' My friends, on the day of Rapture, fly up with the Lord. Don't choose to burn in hell where it's even hotter than molten steel. . . ." His eyes bugged out like a mad man, his big, muscled arms flailing and his feet dancing. But we didn't hear anything after his molten steel image but my voice screaming, detached in some mysterious way from my racing mind.

I couldn't bear the picture of my parents lost forever in a pool of burning metal. I could hear Rhett's voice trembling when he quit his last job, telling Mama, "You git up on one o' them beams and try to handle an ingot of steel hotter 'n hell fire with a hangover. Then we can talk about who's lazy and sorry, by God!"

My worries went haywire. What if my future was a walk on a narrow beam over an open-hearth furnace? What if I slipped and found myself crashing down on the day of Rapture? In the movies, *rapture* meant something romantic, but there was nothing romantic about Brother Billy's rapture.

Even as a baby, ever since I could remember, I'd held my nose against the stench of thick, sulfurous smoke from Sloss Furnace that belched into the sky like an infernal monster. Lucinda always whispered as we passed the stinking mist, "Did you fart?"

My revulsion at the odor rivaled my attraction to the bright stream of melting steel that poured like liquid sun, a blinding molten light. The odor was always there but the shimmering, mysterious stream of steel hotter than fire, we only saw when they poured a fresh ladle. It had always seemed supernatural somehow, certainly not anything connected with human beings that I knew had sinned. I let the piercing scream struggling in my throat free again and again.

"Pearl, take her outside, honey," Rhett said, his Adam's apple working hard. Sweat popping out across his brow, he locked eyes with mine for an instant in which I knew that he knew my thoughts. His dark eyes seemed on fire, melting before me.

The preacher, in rhythmic gasps, continued, "Brothers and sisters, Satan is a clever serpent. He comes to us in all disguises, but we can stomp on him and purify ourselves again." His voice softened to a whisper, "If you have slipped and fell, won't you come tonight and accept forgiveness for your sins. Won't you come?"

My mother slung her purse over one shoulder and me over the other while the girls sang, "O Lamb of God, I Come." Faces in the choir glowed, their mouths making O's like baby birds ready for a worm. Then I saw Rhett's sturdy, broad shoulders making their way to the altar. Lucinda's golden hair shone like a halo when she was left at her seat alone. As she turned to glance in our direction, I saw that her lip was poked out as Mama would say "far enough to ride to Chicago on."

Outside the tent, the spillover crowd listened with a hunger I didn't understand to the orgasmic rhythm of the preacher's voice. Mama's eyes bugged out. She held me tight like she thought I was possessed by demons, her heels clomping on the pavement toward the parking lot on the hill. She set me down on the hood of our truck and shook me, "I want to know what's wrong, baby. I can't help you if I don't know what's making you scream like this. Please, now, try to tell Mama." She strained to soothe, but a desperate, shrill embarrassment cracked her voice.

I didn't know how to tell her what was wrong but sobbed

more, my head cushioned on her soft, wet bosom. My hair stuck to my eyes. The girls' choir droned, "I was sinking deep in sin far from the peaceful shore."

My whole body shook with the terror of sinking deep in sin, trapped eternally in a pool of molten steel. Or of trying to free those fallible adults in my life from such a fate.

"Mama," I finally sputtered, "if God is Love, how come He lets things happen that hurt so bad?"

Eyes brimming, she looked as if I'd slapped her. She recovered quickly though and answered in resignation, "I don't know, Hon, but we don't question the Lord."

"Why?" I cried, half expecting her usual *Because I said so*. She glanced behind her toward the tent, then scrambled in her purse for a Pall Mall. When she struck the match letting off the sulphuric smell, I sobbed again.

Mama looked toward the hilltop where a crowd had gathered to watch the healing part of the service. She glanced toward the quad where a gaggle of girls scurried toward a dormitory. Mama's troubled eyes looked back down the hill toward the circus tent. Two of the girls giggled, pointing toward us. I wondered if Mama recognized the gold satin uniforms, too, when she pulled me closer to her soft, firm breast and held me tighter. Her dress smelled like ginger snaps.

THE DARLING BUDS OF MAY

We enter darkness in Oxford, Mississippi, only three years after Faulkner's death, arriving for the Southern Literary Festival. Doc, our favorite teacher who's young and "with it," comes to deliver the bad news. He smokes a long, slender pipe; the tobacco smells like rich chocolate. "We've decided that students are not to leave the motel," he warns each face answering the six doors we have blocked. He eyes me slyly when I balk.

Wynette, my roommate, and I head for the square almost immediately. She throws a sweater across her shoulders, covering her ample cleavage. "Some things you gotta keep under wraps," she grins, mimicking a redneck voice. The gleaming white courthouse is stark against the quiet square, only a few dim lights visible from the shops and restaurants. A small group of men gathered on the steps talk softly. The rhythmic sound of their stories interspersed with muffled laughter is haunting, as if we've happened on Faulkner's cronies.

When we pick up the scent of Doc's pipe, we follow it to a white lattice gazebo. I parody a Southern belle, batting my lashes, "Fancy meeting you here."

"I won't tell if you won't," he says, his twinkling eyes the color of strong tea. "Wanna walk out toward Rowan Oak?" he asks. Of course, we do. The three of us walk along the edge of the road, facing the lights of occasional cars. An old Nash Rambler creaks toward us, swerves slightly in our direction. After passing us, the driver's pencil-thin neck cranes our way as he looks back. We see the fierce red glow of a cigarette under a baseball cap from the back window like a surreal traffic light warning us to stop.

I shiver, not sure whether it's the night air or fear. "Wonder where Faulkner got his Snopes inspiration," I say to the tail lights that slowly disappear ahead of us beyond the black web of privet hedge along the road.

We have reached the edge of the drive where tall, shapely pines line the path to Faulkner's higher ground. There are no lights, but we see the silhouette of the majestic house in the background. The four columns across the first floor are silvered by the full moon like the thick blanket of grass in front of them.

"Even without that car creeping around here, I think we should head back, girls," Doc says firmly, his voice rich like sorghum syrup.

"I feel intrusive, as if Faulkner's spirit lingers on the grounds," I tell him, rubbing the stiff bumps along my naked arms. Doc takes my arm and hooks it under his. The warmth of his body stirs me.

Wynette cracks only one joke, her voice just shrill enough to reveal her uneasiness. "Hell, I wish that Rambler would come back. I wanted to see what ol' Flem looks like." We titter nervously. She adds, "It's hard to separate what you've imagined from what you're seeing now. Know what I mean?"

"Yeah," I say softly into the honeysuckle fragrance that surrounds us. Silently, we walk back. "Good night ladies," Doc says at our door.

"See you in the morning, Doc," Wynette answers.

"Yeah," I echo softly. His eyes linger for a moment. "Wanna

come in?" I whisper.

"I'd never want to leave," he answers. "Besides, people talk. Maybe we can cook steak at my place when we get back Saturday night, just the two of us."

"Great," I smile and close the door, relieved that Wynette's face is covered with Noxzema and she's lost inside the sound of running water. I can't really talk to anybody about what I feel for this man.

Next morning, when we register on campus, we are greeted by warm, soft-spoken women who offer us coffee from silver urns and home-made biscuits on china plates thin enough to see through. Our host welcomes us with gentle grey eyes the color of his elegant silk tie. The glow of hospitality lifts my spirits, reminds me of the part of Southern heritage I'm proud of. Then we go with a horde of students to Rowan Oak.

A small group of black students hang back as we saunter across the lawn, and I whisper to Wynette, "I didn't know this conference was integrated, did you?"

"Nah. Never thought about it," she says, checking out the guys who line up at the entrance to the house.

A couple of professors, jabbering in harsh tones that tell me they aren't Southern, hold forth. The tall, thin man tells his students, "It's clear that we're fortunate to be seeing Faulkner's home, ya know. It isn't open to the public yet because the university has just begun the tedious process of restoring the place. It certainly needs it!" Nose tilted and mouth twisted, he looks at the faded walls, the peeling paint.

A soft-spoken woman with clear, steady eyes welcomes us and asks that we please not touch things since they have not yet sealed the walls where Faulkner outlined *A Fable.* "You're welcome to look all you like," she smiles, "just don't touch."

The professors continue to compete for attention. Now, it's time for the short, squatty woman to show off her knowledge. "We must never forget this!" she exclaims. "Look where the author outlined the book that won the Pulitzer! A fine book, indeed!" She points toward the scribbled wall as if they are her words while she shrieks toward her students. My eyes seek out Doc's amber gaze, and we smile. He told our class just last week how little Faulkner liked that novel compared to the others he'd written.

When we come downstairs, I am drawn to the old-fashioned telephone, then the numbers written on the wall. I fight my fingers, wanting to trace the numbers and somehow connect, in a personal way, to the writer who scribbled them. No sooner have I stifled the temptation than I see the short, squatty woman eye the wall. "Oh, look. . . " she screeches.

I open the back door and make a beeline to the yard where it's quiet, untouched. I inhale the sweetness of morning air, hear a sparrow in the oak tree, and relax. I walk to the edge of the thick, emerald grass, then hang over a fence. Thinking of Sam Fathers, I study the shack's striations: silver with brown streaks flowing into shades of mud, nutmeg and rust.

I am shocked out of my reverie when I see a little girl bang the front door as she comes out. People still live there! I fight my hand again to keep it from flying toward my mouth. *Intrusive* wasn't strong enough to describe what I felt stumbling into the life of a child who lives inside a shack and gawking at her as if she were in a museum.

I smile feebly at the girl, try to think of something to say. She looks at her feet for an instant before she makes her way toward a sleepy-eyed mule. She talks softly to the animal, then turns back toward me. Her eyes look beyond me toward the clear, blue sky overhead.

Doc waits at the screen door. "I decided it's more of an intrusion to gawk at living people than a ghost," I tell him. I know by his eyes I don't have to explain.

Quite by chance, students from Tougaloo College park their van next to us and pile out. Their skin tones range from deep ebony to golden honey, their eyes conveying various stages of fear and courage. As we make our way down the tree-lined walkway to a reception, the two groups begin to loosely merge. We feel the tension in the air, the suffocating racist cloud like acrid smoke. My quivering voice betrays me the way it does when I sit beside a black stranger on the city bus, trying to appear nonchalant. "Enjoy seeing Yoknapatawpha?" I ask a heavy girl with high cheekbones who looks more like a woman, huge breasts already sagging.

"Oh yeah," she answers, her voice strong, confident. After that, we don't talk, but continue walking along together. I don't even know I'm "marching." Neither does she, I figure, but we know enough to be wary. We both tighten and exchange a worried glance when a frat man, hanging over a balcony, taunts us.

"Where y'all goin', gals?" snarls a tall, thin boy with a close crew cut the color of carrots. His pals crowd around, apparently glad someone has initiated more than glaring. Most of them are bare-chested, sloshing cups of beer like sacred bounty. In a slow, cultivated voice—deep as a river—a freckled boy asks, "What you doin' with that nigger, honey? You just need some excitement."

"I got what she needs! I got something real excitin' for that white girl," another boy slurs to a chorus of laughter.

I feel my heart accelerate, my neck and face redden. I glance behind me to be sure Doc and Wynette are not far away. They walk together, both faces masking emotion. I'm in that dream where you're trying to scream but no sound comes. My brain won't work fast enough to match the arrogance of the boys. I clear my throat, hating the fear that makes it hard to pry my jaws open enough to say what comes to me, "Up yours!"

The girl next to me says, "Don't say another word. Just keep walkin'." Her breathing is heavy now with the strain of carrying extra weight; otherwise she emanates serenity. I hold my breath, quicken my pace and look straight ahead. I always thought I'd have a chance to get psyched up to manage something like this. I hadn't marched in Birmingham, hadn't gone to Selma. I just carried out my private ritual of integrating the city buses, those smelly cramped arenas for blue-collar workers. Facing cocky college boys demands more courage. We are heavily outnumbered by these leering monsters. It astonishes me that some of them are so handsome, yet capable of such meanness.

I realize that this raw, unfinished swagger of college boys is partly what attracts me to an older man. I escape the fear by fantasizing, remembering Doc's smoldering side-long glances in the car all the way to Mississippi. I erase the hell around me

by remembering his lips on mine, the sweet forbidden rela-
tionship. Our conversations were innocent enough initially,
but my hunger for that intense communication cannot be
called innocent. The eyes. I center on his eyes, their mystery
flooding my head with memories and fantasies of future en-
counters. By the time we reach the banquet hall, I have almost
forgotten the presence of danger. Mouth twitching, I mutter
to my ally, "See you later."

"Yeah," is all she answers, the poker face replaced now by
a face of fear as she heads toward friends who wait for her
and I join my buddies who are buzzing about our abuse.

Wynette rode all the way to Tupelo that night with a boy
from Memphis to get some booze, which Doc seemed eager
to share. We sit by the pool until everyone disappears but the
two of us. He slaps at a mosquito on his arm, its blood running
down the vein in his forearm. He makes a smoke ring that
floats above the smoldering eyes and says, "I've never asked a
student out ... before."

I take his hand, place it close to my heart. We have known
each other over a year, but we've only been out together a few
times. He stunned me the first night, "I think I'm falling in love
with you," he whispered into the back of my neck—sharp,
blinding lights exploding throughout my being. Speechless, I
held on tight, but couldn't bring myself to say the words. Tonight, fed by the town's mystique and bonded by that "march"
we made down fraternity row, I murmur, "I felt your strength
behind me when those guys jeered."

He responds, through puffs of pipe smoke in the humid

air, "I was proud of you, afraid, but proud. I wanted to knock hell out of those arrogant bastards, but it would have diminished the dignity two women rising above trash. Besides, that gave me an excuse not to get beat up."

I am drawn to those merry eyes, so brooding a second ago. Surrendering to the pounding waterfall inside my throat, I utter the words at last, "I love you."

He squeezes my hand. We gaze into the pool of blue as if it were an ocean of future—both afraid to look at each other, afraid of the intensity of the moment.

When I unlock the door, I hear Wynette snoring. She sprawls on the bed, taking up three quarters of it. Her golden hair has a sheen even in the darkness. Her voluptuous breasts spill out of the thin cotton gown that fit her last semester. I shake her, ignoring her boozy breath. "Wake up. I have something to tell you," I begin. We talk into the night, then fall into a deep, peaceful, sleep.

Next morning, we learn that somewhere across town the kids from Tougaloo slept fitfully. Someone set their van on fire. Probably not one of them had the energy left to fall in love. Then I remembered the look in the heavy girl's eyes, the one who told me to keep quiet and keep walking. She would. Somehow she would have the energy. Like the little girl outside the shack, she would look beyond this into the blue sky.

FEELING SALTY

Peanuts growing in dirt the color of blood dotted the endless green countryside. Nick raced through the rich, flat farmland, wind from the open window whipping his hair. He could still get to the bus terminal on time, though it had taken an extra half hour to talk the old farmer into a good deal on the potting soil.

He topped the bridge, caught the first sight of the indigo water stretching out to meet the clouds at the edge of the sky. He inhaled a whiff of salt air. Though he'd been here for months, his heart still beat faster at the sight of the Gulf of Mexico from this hilltop. The vast blue quietly lapped the shoreline, its sand like sugar, it was so soft and white.

He pulled into the bus terminal just in time for his son's arrival. Nick felt a prick of disappointment when Tony rolled his eyes in adolescent disdain. Tony's tousled hair brushed the frame of the door when he stepped off the bus. Nick waved to Tony, who smiled in spite of his attempt to appear aloof, the even white teeth like pearls against the full lips. Nick, suddenly warm, felt a tightness in his chest under the tapered denim shirt. He made his way through the crowd to the boy, took the duffel and reached for a hug at the same time. When he saw Tony shrink back from the show of affection, he said, "Give me five."

Tony half-heartedly slapped his palm. They moved quickly to the truck to avoid the hot, smelly gush of exhaust fumes of a new bus arriving from Atlanta. When Nick fished in his tight jeans pocket for the keys his knuckles caught. Must be the middle-aged spread beginning, he thought. Relieved to be away from the bus terminal, Nick headed back to the beach. The ample muscle in his forearm strained as he rolled down the window.The slap of fresh air rushed in again, pushing Nick's plaid shirt away from his damp, hairy chest.

"So, how's it going?" he asked the boy.

Tony switched on the radio, fiddling with the stations."Fine," he answered absently. He found a rock station, turned the volume up too loud for talk and settled into his own fog.

Nick tried again,"I know you'll enjoy crabbing here. Hope you'll like the work; branching off into horticulture and trying to keep up the construction business, too, is more than one man can handle. Of course, I'll pay you well." He could see Tony wasn't listening. Might as well let it pass. For a while, they drove on without conversation down the front beach road where high-rises daily eroded the beach.

"That wasn't even here last spring,"Tony marveled, pointing to a development of pink stucco houses with terra cotta roofs.

"The growth in this area is incredible," Nick answered. "Those who aren't building are remodeling. See that old 50's cottage on the right? I watched 'em slap a coat of salmon paint on and build that prissy porch on the roof. It used to be great, had a wrap-around screen porch where my fishing buddies played poker at night without getting whopped by mosquitoes." He noticed the boy had tuned him out again, staring out to sea—his green eyes cloudy as a margarita against the dark face lashed by the lush ponytail.

"Yep," Tony muttered, "all those old 1960s cedar places

puttin' on a new face."

Tony's squeaky voice startled Nick. The boy had been listening! Finally, Tony interrupted the long, awkward silence that
followed by drumming on the dashboard and singing along,
"Pump up the volume, pump up the volume," just before Nick
turned off the highway onto the long driveway lined with cy-
press trees.

The Victorian tower came into view as the driveway curved
toward the water. Nick glanced to see if he could read his
son's face. Poker smooth. Tony refused to appear impressed
by the lavish home from the outside; his sneer at the interior
was worse.

The boy followed him down the hall to the guest room,
which was sparsely furnished with a single bed, a stack of plastic crates in primary colors and a mirror propped against the
wall. Tony looked around, sullen. It was clear from his wide,
broad frame that Tony would be strong, formidable even, but
the muscle had just begun to fill in. Everything about him was
tentative, unformed yet.

"It's fine," Tony said, scowling. "Suits me." He opened the
closet and said, "Nice. Big." He slipped the duffel in and shut
the door.

Nick said, "Hey, man, let's check out the beach."

Tony brightened like a lamp turned on at dusk. At the edge
of the path, waves crashed the shore, clouds overhead threat-
ening, heavy, as if they'd been sketched with charcoal across
the sky, then smudged so dark they were almost black. Late
afternoon thunderstorms settled in every day now. "Check out
this pier," Nick said.

He squatted, pulled the trap out of the water proudly. He'd painted the chicken wire black to prevent rust. "This morning, I decided chicken might attract more crab, but it didn't work. I've checked three times now. It was expensive bait compared to that old smelly fish I usually buy for a dollar a bag," Nick griped, mostly to himself.

He smirked at Tony's wide eyes and open mouth, his fascination with the buoys bobbing across the water's surface. He grumbled, "You got to get up mighty early to compete with the Vietnamese."

"Look at all those colors, man," Tony squealed.

"There must be hundreds of 'em," Nick complained.

Tony shook his head. "They got a right to be here. Same as you."

Nick busied himself with the bait. "Let's throw some smelly fish heads in. Give 'em these spines and guts. Maybe we'll have some fat ones by night fall." He slipped on a pair of bright yellow gloves and tossed a pair to Tony. "You have to use gloves nowadays."

"We gonna catch AIDS from the Vietnamese?" Tony chuckled.

"I'm serious, man," Nick warned. "There's a deadly bacterial infection in the gulf that attacks sores on hands, arms, legs and feet."

Tony ambled down the pier and pulled up a trap. He tossed fish skin carelessly toward it, spilling more than he used. Nick yanked the bag and finished filling the trap himself when he saw that Tony had stuffed the gloves in his pocket. The boy stuffed his hands in his back pockets, his back toward Nick who winced when he saw the "cleavage" at his son's waist-band. The pale skin contrasted with the smooth even suntan. The older man was grateful for the silence, which gave him a chance to get hold of the irritation he felt.

After the strain passed, Nick told his son, "Ma Marta won't use a trap. She uses a string with a chicken neck attached to it so she can lure those suckers toward her net."

They both laughed softly. "Gives her more control," Tony muttered, wiping the sweat from his forehead.

"You and Ma still fish a lot?" Nick asked.

Tony chewed on his nail, looking away. Nick waited for the answer. "Not so much," Tony finally said, his voice high-pitched. The confession brought misery to the boy's eyes, cloudy again. Brows knitted in a frown, he added, "You know, she's my grandma. Besides, she's so bossy. It's just not like it used to be."

"I know," Nick sympathized, "she raised me too, don't forget. I never would have wished it on you, never wanted to leave your mom. I just screwed up. That's all."

Nick attempted to lighten the moment, "But, what the hell, you're here now, and we're gonna have a great time."

Tony's mask of boredom was in place again.

In the afternoon, they drove over to the dilapidated pottery shop, which looked seedier than Nick had realized. His pride in the project wilted with each fresh realization that the place was a dump. The rotten frame of the screen door squeaked, and the dirt floor seemed an affectation which made Nick feel foolish.

He could hear the hollow ring in his voice as he intro-
duced his son, feeling more like an imposter than a father, "Tony,
I'd like you to meet Wes, my partner." He still couldn't get used
to thinking of Wes as his partner in this venture.

"Hey," Tony said, shaking Wes's hand but looking away. Nick
settled some figures with Wes, scribbling in the ledger they
kept, and filed several receipts. Then he followed his son toward the back hallway.

Nick lectured as soon as they reached the back door, "Son,
you always look a man in the eye when you shake his hand ..."

"Too bad nobody's been around to teach me tricks like
that," Tony said, reaching for a bag of potting soil from Nick's
truck. "Better hustle," the boy added, "we've got a lot to un-
load." Tony was sullen, quiet, as the two of them worked, grunt-
ing and sweating in the thick, humid heat.

Back inside, Tony was rude, withdrawn, poking his head in
cabinets and exploring dusty shelves. Wes tried too hard to
put the boy at ease, insisting that he have a cup of tea, something Nick himself was just beginning to tolerate from Wes.
"You offer teenagers a Coke," he snapped, hating the all-know-
ing tone he'd picked up.

Wes grinned, "I wish I had some coke to offer him." Tony
grinned back at him as if the pony tails drew the two of them
closer than Nick was to either one--camaraderie, fellow rebels
against the world, horses' asses, he concluded. Nick practiced
the imagery he'd been taught in therapy for attention deficit
disorder as soon as he felt the anger twist his stomach. The
mood swings, the overreactions were the worst part of it. He
pictured Wes and Tony as young innocent boys riding bikes

against traffic, then Wes with a clown's face. The images eased the tightness in his gut, brought a smile to his face instead.

Nick's mind snapped back to the moment when Wes offered Tony a cigarette. The boy, looking at Wes blankly, said, "No thanks, man." Nick started to protest; a man shouldn't offer a kid tobacco. He changed the subject instead, a vague uneasiness settling into his stomach.

It was not until Alyce stopped by and raved about the pots Wes made for the dill plants that Tony showed any real interest in the project. Nick admired his son for his restraint about Alyce, who was a knockout—tall, blonde and leggy. She was a good ten years older than the boy, but, of course, that didn't matter. Nick could see the boy was aware of her sex appeal, but he didn't pant like a puppy. Tony's eyes lingered just long enough on her round, firm breasts, jiggling in the tee shirt. Then the boy, suddenly all arms and legs, moved over to Wes's weathered worktable. He became absorbed in the pots Alyce admired.

Alyce followed him, pointing toward her favorites with her flashy red nails and gushing over the colors. "I had a rough afternoon with Ms. Brasfield, wish I could paint that old grouch's hair mauve," she said, winking at Tony. She sat down, took her shoes off and rubbed her feet, the crotch of her panties visible in the short skirt. She sensed Nick's attention, crossed her smooth, silky legs, and pouted toward him, "My feet are killing me. They don't warn you about that in cosmetology college."

Nick felt naked in his hungry response to Alyce, then relieved that Tony and Wes seemed unaware of the chemistry that hung in the air heavy as Alyce's scent of gardenia. He moved behind the counter, looked away toward the guys. Tony was fascinated, watching Wes take a blob of cold, slippery clay and flop it on the wheel. Set low to the ground, the potter's wheel made Wes hunch his broad shoulders, the way Nick's mother hovered over her sewing machine. Tony's eyes followed Wes's hands, which caressed the pot as he shaped it, the wobbly wheel moving faster as Wes's legs pumped harder.

Wes told Tony, "I can do this all day whether I get paid or not, but there's more money in making molds." Scooting over to make a place for Tony to sit, Wes showed him the mold for the rosemary plants.

"Oh, I get it," Tony brightened. "Rosemary Beach souvenirs. Cool!" The boy shot his father a look of admiration.

Nick warmed to the recognition as much as Wes. "Hell, we gonna sell 'em as Christmas trees!"

"It might be Christmas before I get all this painted," Wes said, feathering the small lines in the wet clay.

Tony blurted, "Let me help paint them. I'll do those little green lines. I like detail stuff like that."

Wes smiled eagerly and handed Tony the stiff brush, "Be my guest, man. You must have been sent by the Universe. I don't have the patience to do delicate work. I like gettin' my hands in the big-ass stuff." He glanced at Alyce who was mixing paint. She shook the paint container hard, making her breasts dance, and smiled knowingly. To nobody in particular, she sang out in a hoarse voice like Kristofferson, "If you're feeling salty, I'm yo' tequila!"

When he picked Tony up after the boy's first full day at the shop, Nick strutted—father proud. Things were going as he'd hoped. He had his boy working for him in a satisfying business, and they were going crabbing after dinner.

When Nick saw Tony's soft eyes locked in concentration at the table, his thick eyelashes almost like a woman's, he felt a warm glow of pride. There was nothing else womanish about Tony; the boy was handsome, solid.

The glow was brief. Nick felt an internal switch shut off when he saw that Tony hadn't touched the rooting project. The boy had painted a whole shelf of pots for Wes, but ignored the African violets Nick had told him to start on first. Nick's disappointment turned quickly to anger, but he tried to avoid feeling anything. He couldn't afford to lose his temper, create a scene. He'd invested a lot in this project.

All he'd told Tony to do was cut the leaves, dip them in rooting hormone and stick them in the dirt. Nick's jaw tightened and his fist clenched involuntarily when he saw the whole area he had set up untouched. Even the book with the instructions he had underlined had not been opened.

"Looks like you guys had a big day," he said sarcastically.

The sarcasm was lost on Wes and Tony. They might as well both have been teenagers. Wes's grin covered his face underneath the thin, sandy hair, "Yeah, man, look at this stuff we made today. Super, ain't it!"

Tony grinned, too, but when he saw Nick's face he looked away, disappeared like a turtle pulling inside a sturdy shell.

Something snapped inside Nick like a streak of lightning.

"Don't start that pouting crap with me, boy," Nick yelled, his voice wild, furious, out of control. He smashed an ashtray on the edge of the counter and kicked a bag of soil, breaking the bag open and spilling dirt everywhere. Only when he threw the book across the room, barely missing the two startled, open mouths, did Nick remember his son was witnessing his outburst.

Nick struggled to calm himself, remembering the doctor's warning. Controlling his temper was vital to improving his mood swings. Waiting until he could think things over worked if he could do it. A big if. He found the broom and dust pan, stooped to clean up his mess. He was grateful when Tony squatted to help.

Wes sat at the potter's wheel, his hands adept in the moist clay. He never looked up, never said a word.

"Well, let's hit the road," Nick said, yawning and stretching, attempting to appear nonchalant.

Tony looked straight through his dad, went back where he'd been sitting, put his brush in the mineral oil and closed the paint. "Whatever," he finally said.

When they got in the truck, Nick started in, "When I tell you to do something and leave you somewhere for nearly eight hours, son, I expect you to do it. You didn't touch those violets, didn't even mention it. No apology. No nothing." Nick's voice rose, his hands shook.

"We just got involved, that's all. Chill out, Dad, I'll get to it tomorrow," Tony said as if it were the least important thing in the world. He turned up the radio.

Nick gripped the steering wheel hard, too hard. Hell, maybe it isn't all that important, he told himself and drove along in silence, trying to take deep rhythmic breaths.

After they grilled hot dogs in the rain, Tony asked if he could use the computer. "Sure," Nick said, "Help yourself."

The boy stayed in front of the screen until bedtime, but he quit pouting. He played games, adjusting colors and shapes for hours. He finally gave it up and watched a couple of innings with Nick, but he talked too much—even with the bases loaded.

"I'm tellin' you, those women in chat groups will say anything! Some old woman crawled all over a girl from Minnesota while ago ..."

"Minnesota, huh?" Nick managed to respond.

"It's an education, man, surfing the net," Tony started.

Nick screamed at the umpire, "What ya doin', man! He was in there!"

Tony left the room without a word, but hell, it was the ninth inning. Nick decided to let the conflict at the shop ride a day and see what happened. He told himself this must be the fatigue guys talk about, being exhausted by teenagers. No physical work he had ever done had made him this tired.

Nick exhaled a sigh, knowing that soon the balloon of elation at seeing his son would be totally flat. The boy must have grown a foot, Nick thought. Unfortunately, so had the ponytail. And Tony wore a large, gold loop earring instead of the stud Nick had managed not to comment on last time.

Nick felt tossed like the crashing waves outside the window, as he lay awake until at least midnight, remembering the morning. The dirty, crowded loading dock had made Nick feel guilty for making Tony ride the bus. It hadn't really occurred to him that he'd feel so protective toward his son until he saw the kind of people who piled out of the bus. A whole new crop of Mexican machismo had emerged since Nick's bus-riding days. Guys with long sideburns who looked like drug smugglers in tight pants and snake skin boots pressed their way through the black matriarchs and the smattering of angry, wiry white folks whose necks jerked like hens at pecking time. No wonder Tony had looked edgy: not a good beginning for the month-long visit.

The boy's chin had a row of small pimples across it, and his hair was oily, darker. Even zits couldn't mar the nearly perfect face, the sea green eyes shocking against the dark skin. He had obviously started shaving and had nicked his chin. Nick ran his palm across his own stubbled cheek, feeling the same high cheekbones under his fuller face.

The sea grew calmer after a brief thunderstorm. Finally, Nick grew calm as well, timing his breathing with the mystery of the sea pounding in his ear.

The next day, the violets got rooted, but, Nick suspected, in haste. When Nick came in, Alyce was painting pots with Tony—transported, an earnest sweetness on her face Nick had never seen before. She sat close to Tony, her breast pressed against his arm. They had an assembly line approach: Wes stacked the pots, Tony painted purple violets, and Alyce painted a band around the top of each pot, a swirl of mauve and purple.

In animated voice, Alyce held forth, "I loved my art classes, made straight A's, but when Daddy got Alzheimer's, my college days were done. Granny laughed when I told her I saw a play about a hairdresser who said doing hair was like sculpture, but it is."

Tony pulled back from her, looked skeptical. His questioning eyes penetrated Alyce's smile. She continued, "Granny didn't trust art much, but she taught me ever' trick in the book about hairstyles."

"Those pots look good," Nick exclaimed. "You two are quite a team."

Alyce turned a puzzled face toward him, her almond-shaped eyes unable to restrain flirtation even in a serious moment. Tony moved away from the girl, cleared his throat. His cheeks were flushed, the same dusty rose of his shirt, which he wore unbuttoned and outside his painters' pants.

Wes let out a whistle. "I have to watch 'em all the time. Can't shut 'em up, but they do turn out the pots, don't they? They're at the same point on the journey, man. How's the greenhouse coming?"

"Almost through," Nick answered.

That night, while Tony tuned into the computer again, Nick rocked in the porch swing, in rhythm with the waves gently lapping the shore. He reviewed the father-son match in his head. His doctor insisted that it would go easier if he thought of the conflict like a tennis match with Tony. Nick didn't like tennis though he had to agree it was a good outlet for his anger. He felt as awkward at tennis as he did at parenting-- both games for the leisure class.

However, when the boy came out on the porch, Nick tried. He whistled softly, "You really get into painting those pots, don't you?"

"Yep, me and Alyce must have done 50 or more this afternoon,"Tony boasted.

"Alyce there that long?" Nick said, raising his eyebrow.

"She comes by there after work all the time now. She really likes to paint." He pulled his father's hair playfully. "Stop snooping. She's Wes's squeeze. We get off on doing that stuff."

"I hope that's all you're getting off on," Nick said, crossing his arms, startled by the tight voice he recognized as his own.

"I don't think you need to worry,"Tony said, his voice flat. No way to read between the lines whether he meant it was none of Nick's business. Then Tony turned his back toward the older man and leaned against the banister, staring up at the hint of a moon—a thin red sliver like a fingernail against the clear, dark sky. It was as if they were momentarily frozen in the dark silence between them. Tony's soft voice broke the spell, "Not to worry," he said, smiling.

Nick attempted to carry it further, "Alyce is a beautiful woman. . . . "

"Yep,"Tony answered, the screen door screeching behind him. Nick heard his heavy footsteps on the stairs above the soft whisper from the waves. He remembered Alyce's saucy eyes when she shook the paint yesterday. He closed his eyes, still rocking. He tasted salt on his lips.

Nick and Tony arrived an hour before Wes, the early morning air cool after a light rain. They worked well together, with Tony cutting the plants and dipping them while Nick packed the soil carefully in the pots. After Wes arrived, Nick teased, "Still keeping Hollywood hours, huh?"

Wes's toothy smile, from a mouth a bit too large for his face, was his only answer. Nick and Wes nailed braces on the worn, sagging display shelves, leaving Tony on his own.

Mid-morning, they drank chicory coffee and munched do-nuts. Nick ate too many of the chocolate ones, which made him sleepy. He stood and stretched, almost reaching the dingy ceiling. He tried not to show his disapproval of the run-down condition of the shop, knowing he had to choose his battles. Before he could finish the thought, he discovered another conflict. Tony had cut several dozen plants, but only potted one.

"What are you doing?" Nick snapped. "I told you to put them in the soil quickly."

"Quick is a relative term," Tony sassed. "It's more efficient this way."

Nick felt his neck stiffen, but he stifled the anger. Might as well cut the boy some slack, he thought, as he stooped to fill the pots with soil.

"Come to Poppa, baby," he said to the cutting. He smiled at Tony who made a gag gesture, his finger pointing to the back of his tongue.

They worked together in comfortable silence until lunch. All three guys inhaled the oyster po' boys Nick brought in, Wes swilling a cold beer with his.

While Wes was taking his siesta, the inevitable 30-minute nap that came with his lunch break, Nick and Tony returned to their work. Nick grunted with satisfaction as he dug into the bag of soil he'd mixed with peat moss. "I love the feel of dirt, that smell."

The boy's voice was strained when he responded, almost shrill, "You know, Dad, I hate that part, getting my hands in that gooky stuff, having that stink inside my fingernails. I'm sorry I haven't been better about it, but I really hate it."

Nick flinched, but he held his automatic anger in check. Since he was a grown man fighting mood swings like an adolescent, maybe he should have patience with a teenager. Tony's high-pitched, rehearsed explanation gnawed at Nick.

He practiced the deep breathing. "Funny how we're so different," he said. "There's nothing I love more than that smelly soil. It takes all kinds."

"Right," Tony answered, a smile playing at the curve of his mouth.

Nick patted the soil, savoring the satisfaction of resisting defensiveness. Doc would call it *really communicating*. He added, "It takes time to get a business up and running. I've been assuming that everybody would do everything. I'm glad you're here, buddy, and willing to help us out." Nick's hands trembled around the cutting. He marveled that such a short utterance left him drained, bone-tired.

That night, walking along the beach after dinner, Nick could see Tony upstairs at the computer screen. The power struggle seemed to dissipate at home where they both went their own way. Though Nick missed the softness of a woman at night, it was a relief to have a son who knew how to stay out of the way. He slept soundly, grateful for a peaceful evening.

He roused Tony early, slapping a pillow in his face. Tony groaned at first but warmed to the pillow fight. Nick told the breathless face under the pillow, "I want to take you out where the bay meets the gulf, where the dolphins swim up to the boat and eat right out of your hand."

Nick stashed the small fish in a cooler at the back of the boat. He let Tony steer along the sandbar where the water was shallow. At first the boy was nervous but he took to the boat like he'd steered it all his life. The water was fairly calm, the waves even. The blues and greens were clear of seaweed, the ocean-bottom formations under them like miniature hills. The beach along both sides of the sandbar glistened, so white it looked like snow piled on the beach in the bright sunlight.

For a brief moment, Nick's son looked like the innocent boy he'd been at eight when wonder was new. The breeze blew the dark curls around Tony's eyes, shaded by a Marlins cap. Mouth ajar, his eyes widened when he spotted the dolphins swimming up to the boat. Tony was entranced by the largest one swimming straight toward them. His knuckles paled as he steered the boat to avoid the dolphin, the waves sloshing.

"Don't worry, son. They know exactly what they're doing," Nick reassured him as he opened the cooler and lifted the iridescent fish, glistening in the sun. The dolphin made an arc of silver as it jumped—mouth open for the fish—so close Nick reached out and patted it. Tony's large eyes—as clear and turquoise as the sea that surrounded him—smiled toward his father. That expression would stay with Nick forever, he knew. They switched the boat off and drifted.

"You know what?" Tony said.

"What?" Nick replied, opening his eyes from a cat nap in the sun.

"I could stay right here forever,"Tony said, trailing his hand in the water.

Nick reached for his other hand and squeezed it.

In some ways, Nick was relieved the month was almost over. Nick had, more than once, smelled pot in the shop when he'd come back from errands. He hadn't said anything, figured it was better not to make too much of it. There was no doubt that Wes and Tony had become close in spite of the attraction between Alyce and Tony. When the four of them decided to have a farewell party at the end of Tony's last day, Nick went out to pick up the food Alyce ordered at the deli.

When he parked at the back of the shop, Nick was startled by the loud music, but more surprised by what he saw from the window. Alyce, with her blouse unbuttoned, was sitting on the counter, her long, tan legs wrapped around Tony's waist, kissing him hard, passionately. Nick moved closer to the window. Now he could see that Tony had his shirt on, but his jeans were around his ankles, his butt grinding like he knew what he was doing. This obviously wasn't the first time.

Nick was astonished at the surge of conflicting emotions he felt—anger, lust, envy, protective rage. Were they crazy? Where the hell was Wes? What would he do if he caught them? Then he saw Wes, sitting in a straight chair tipped back against the wall not five feet from Tony and Alyce, an insane grin plastered on his face. He sucked on the joint hanging from his mouth. His arms filled with deli trays, Nick kicked the door open with a loud crash.

"What the hell is going on here?" Nick demanded. "This is

my son, not some damn drifter you two picked up on the beach!" He plopped the food on the counter and swept the freshly painted pots off with a loud crash.

"Hold on, man," Wes said, getting out of his chair and ambling toward Nick, his African daishiki almost to his knees like a damned dress. "We were just having a little fun. No harm done, man. It's just good karma."

Alyce pulled at the short skirt as if it would cover anything, her eyes all pupil. "I live by the pleasure principle," she hissed. "You oughtta try it sometimes."

"Don't talk down to me, you little slut! I knew about pleasure when your fat ass was in diapers," Nick barked.

"That's my woman you're talking to," Wes screamed, pushing Nick against the wall.

Nick was powerless over the rage that exploded inside him. He punched Wes in the eye with a fist that frightened even him with its fury. Wes crumpled to the floor, blood running from his nose. He scraped translucent flakes of skin from his hand when he tried to break the fall.

"You're making a fool of yourself, old man," Alyce screamed. "It was your son who instigated every bit of it, your baby boy who talked us hicks into *a ménage a trois*! Godamighty, take a look at him. Who the hell wouldn't? Where've you been while he's been making notes on the Internet, diddling yourself?"

Nick yanked Alyce's hair, twisted her toward him. He hadn't been this furious since Tony's mother.

"Dad," Tony said, his eyes pleading while his strong, young frame lunged toward them. Nick froze when he saw pain pucker the boy's face, the same face he'd horrified years ago when he'd slapped Tony's mother so hard he cut her lip. Suddenly, Nick realized how painful this was for his son on so many levels. Surely that was more important than the anger Nick felt. He pulled strength from an undiscovered depth inside his soul, slowing his heavy breathing. He let go of the silky blonde hair, which Alyce tossed back in place with a shake of her head.

"Hell," Nick muttered after a minute, "I guess I shouldn't have been surprised. You lay down with dogs, you get up with fleas."

Tony and Alyce tittered, Tony's laughter on the edge of hysteria. Wes was still floating somewhere, his eyes unfocused. Once Alyce brought a wet cloth and pressed it over the swollen eye, he came around fairly quickly.

Nick drove home in silence, noting that the boy's misty eyes were not dilated. When they got out of the truck, Nick struggled to get the right tone for the question he had to ask. "Just tell me one thing, Tony. Have you been doing drugs with those two?"

Tony shot back with amazing passion. "Quit fantasizing, Dad, you're not gonna find any weed on me. I'm not that stupid. I know what it did to you. I watched it turn you into a wife-beater; at least I'm not into that."

Nick winced. He leaned against the fender of the truck and turned his creased forehead to the sky as if pleading for answers. He asked the boy, "What came over you? What were you thinking, Tony? Getting involved with both of them?"

Tony shrugged his shoulders, "Get a grip, Dad." He added, over his shoulder, as he slammed the screen door, "At least, catch up with the times, for Christ's sake."

On the way to the bus, Nick stopped at an oyster bar over-looking the ocean. The two men ate raw oysters and watched the dolphins swim up to the window, frolicking in the warm emerald water.

"I'll never forget the day we fed the dolphins," Tony said.

"It was a good day, wasn't it," Nick responded, the knot in his throat working.

Tony looked his father in the eye. "Thank you," he said simply.

Nick's eyes stung with tears, his attachment to the boy surprising. He shook his head, sighed deeply and said, "Oh yeah, by the way, here's something for you." He slipped a package of condoms across the table. "Ever since you've been here, I've been trying to find the right time to talk to you about these, explain things."

Tony rolled his eyes, then smiled. Wordless, they watched a pair of dolphins chase each other through the salty green-ness.

SEEING IT THROUGH

I've always been a good natured, easy-going woman, but I don't take no crap either. As long as things are rocking along smoothly, I'm easy to get along with, but my friends and my husband Hooty know better than to cross me.

At first I laughed about the doctor's office not being able to find a pot for a woman to pee in. My doctor is one of those fools moving into the north end of the county, more interested in them prissy horses they raise than anything else.

In fact, ever since I've been seeing him for my rheumatism, I've noticed that he talks about his horses more than my problems. I figured it was my good-natured way that made him do it, so I smiled and listened good and secretly started keeping score, tallying his comments. Right now it's me: 11, horses: 32.

But lately, I haven't had time to keep score. One day last February Dr. Alvarez was talking away while I was trying to tell him about these strange little spells I'd been having. I get so hot it feels like my hair is on fire, which I know sounds like the change, but I also get so cold, I mean so cooooooooooold it feels like all the heat is going right out the top of my head or the tips of my toes.

That's how come I started wearin' these hats. Most of 'em are baseball caps, but my favorite hat come from a little man who died over at the nursing home where I work as a cleanup woman. His wife give it to me along with several pairs of his flannel pj's that I'm crazy about, but that hat is the stuff. It's bright blue, almost purple. She said it come from Paris, France. It's the style like they used to wear during World War I. I don't know what you call it, but I like to wear it cocked to one side. Hooty says I wear all my hats like a French whore.

So, I'm sitting in the doctor's office explaining to him, wrapped up in a wool scarf and got that hat cocked just right. He said real casually while he was writing in the folder like he could care less, "There's a test we could run, might tell us a little more."

The girl out at the desk, the one with all that gook on her eyes who's dressed fit to kill like she's goin' somewhere else in about two minutes, told me it was a 24-hour urine test. She told me just when to start, gave me a little diet and all.

The nurse was a boy or at least partly boy if you know what I mean, kinda prissy. He brought me a thing out that looked like a urinal and told me to urinate in that thing every time I had to pee for 24 hours. I asked him how he thought I could, and he started stammering around. Then the made-up girl started giggling.

"See, she knows what I mean," I said. But he still looked blank.

"Use your imagination, Kevin," she said ducking her head and looking up at him all cute like.

I could hear myself gettin' loud, "Dearie," I said to him, "some of us have to squat to pee. I can't stand up and fit myself into that thang. I need one of those little round containers that fits under the toilet seat."

His puffy, pale face just got pinker and those long eyelashes actually started fluttering. I felt sorry for him since he was so stupid. So just to help him figure it out I said, "I can't sit down on the toilet and hold this thing up under me; there's not enough room in the toilet even if I did want to make such a mess."

He finally got it. The girl assured me she would find the right *receptacle* as she called it and get back to me. A couple of weeks passed and the spells had let up some, so I just plain forgot about it.

Then it got to be summer, and Hooty had started swearin' like he always does, how we couldn't live in this oven of a trailer another year while I'd be settin' there freezin', with three sweaters on and my hat. I decided it was time I called the make-up queen. She said she hadn't been able to locate a receptacle, that I should call their office in Birmingham.

When I did the girl there told me to call the horsey office, but I told her, "Hold on here, girl. You the one gettin' paid; you call them and take care of this, and I mean business."

It was along about then that Hooty started to get that mean look on his face when the subject of my doctor came up. In September when the time came for my follow-up appointment, I realized that in all the excitement about the receptacle, both the girl and I had forgot to set up an appointment, which was already overdue. At that point, the first time I could see the horse's rear: December 5.

"Well," I sneered, "at least this oughtta give y'all enough time to get that test done."

It hurt me to look in her eyes with all that mascara caked on them, so heavy. Looks like she could've seen her eyes were red as road maps, prob'ly allergic to all that gook. I fixed her with my gaze: "I came up here in person to set up my appointment so I could pick up that pee pot." (By now I enjoyed watching their shock. They felt sorry for me, thought I didn't know any better ... like I couldn't learn to say *receptacle*.)

"I'm sorry, Ms. Sims," she said, putting her claws—painted a dark Satanic looking color—out to pat me on the shoulder. I can't stand that little old lady treatment, so I brushed her hand away. She went on, her voice acting like her hand was still patting me on the shoulder, "I have ordered it from a special lab and it should be here soon."

Well, then to top it off, finally in November when I called to see what was holding her up she said, "Oh, it's been here for weeks. I thought you'd come to pick it up."

"What's wrong with the U. S. Mail?" I asked. "Or Alexander Graham Bell's invention, the plain simple telephone that doctors once used to call their patients?"

Then she said, "Could you please hold?" and snapped the connection, never gave me a chance to answer. Of course, she assumed the answer was yes I can wait all day. She came back on all cheery, like it was good news:"Doc said maybe you should just wait till he sees you again, maybe you don't need this test after all since it's been so long already."

I said, "You tell him that the symptoms we talked about are a whole lot worse and I don't need to go to medical school to know that something's wrong and I still need whatever it was he wanted to test." So they did the test, naturally.

Who do you think had to see to the pot's delivery?! Yours truly. Since I couldn't get up there during the week, they had to hide the pot in the bushes for me one Saturday when me and Hooty were going into town.

Then, when I saw the horse doctor, a full ten months after my last visit, he said very casually, "The test came back normal, but you could still have a carcinoid tumor. There's another test that goes into more detail."

My heart stopped, but I tried not to show it. Tumor. I was not about to admit that I wasn't sure what carcinoid meant, but I knew what carcinoma meant and carcinogenic. Well I sorta knew.

I had Mama with me. I couldn't think about all that right then. Hooty had said we could take Mama to her favorite restaurant, a "joint" that makes good greens and fried okra. The food used to be better till they moved up to this end of the county to serve all them Yankees and yuppies who don't really know how to appreciate good food.

I didn't mention anything to Mama and Hooty at first. We just went on to dinner, and then I told them I had to go to a specialist, but I didn't mention tumor in front of Mama. That night after Hooty was asleep I got up and went to the front of the trailer and looked up carcinoid in the dictionary, but it wasn't in there. I found carcinogenic and carcinoma and had myself a good cry. Ten months wasted from sheer stupidity. I was just numb, but I didn't know nothing yet. I had just begun to jump through the hoops.

Dr. Alvarez could call himself South American if he wanted to, but he looked Mexican to me. He was big and fat and sloppy and his skin glistened like he'd just rubbed Crisco all over himself. I was always saying I wouldn't buy a used car from this man, but then I was letting him see after the best engine I had—me. To give him credit, he could be nice and gentle once I started pushing for information. He said he couldn't say for sure what the problem was, but that carcinoid tumors were not malignant. I sighed, relieved. Then he said he wanted to do the urine test over and do it a little differently, wanted me to come downtown to the big office. I tried to tell Hooty how nice Dr. Alvarez could be when he took the time, but he didn't seem to hear me.

Hooty took a day of sick leave, insisted on it. He put on them snakeskin boots and strapped his pistol to his holster like he was going to war. When we got off the elevator, he set off the beeper and the security guards searched him.

"Wait just a minute, buddy," the elderly man in uniform said when the beeper went off.

Hooty reddened, but he wasn't about to tell them about the gun, so they frisked him. He enjoyed making them find it, started grinning all over himself.

The elderly man said, "You got a permit for this thing, friend?"

Hooty showed him the little card he carried around, showing that he was a volunteer deputy. Then he swaggered a little and said, "There's been so much trouble downtown lately, all them drive-by shootin's, we couldn't believe it. Wadn't no way we was coming downtown without some protection. We watch the 10 o'clock news ever night, by damn."

The guard was looking sorta funny by then because Hooty had started to get that mean look. "Well," he said, "you're welcome to protect yourself and this lovely little lady all you want to once your business in the hospital's over, but we have a policy here that nobody can take a weapon into the hospital."

"We ain't goin' to no hospital, she's got a appointment with the doctor, that's all," Hooty explained, grinning now.

"Yessir, I see," said the guard, "but since the hospital is connected to the research wing, we just hold weapons here. It's the same difference as leaving your car keys for valet parking."

"Yeah, but see, I don't use valet parking, buddy, never have," Hooty said.

"Hooty," I interrupted. "Give him the gun. We gonna be late."

"Aw hell," he said, "ahhhiiight."

We made our way through the lobby of what Hooty called the country club and finally found Dr. Alvarez's office. Hooty kept grumbling all through the hallways about how they musta thought he was Dr. Kevorkian or something or maybe one of these guys bent on shootin' abortionists. "Hey, that's a way to show 'em some excitement, ain't it?" he said, jabbing me in the side too hard. "Ask 'em where the abortion clinic is and flash this holster." He was patting the empty holster, laughing strange.

I tried to distract him. I had read in the paper that some famous Chinese man with a name like *I Am Pee* had designed the building. It had a huge fountain in the front that I thought looked just like a man peeing, without a receptacle, of course. Sorta like the way men like to pee in the yard I figured.

Hooty just gaped at it, craning his neck over the railing. "What you call this thang, a atrium?" he asked. "Reckon how much money they waste a month on the water bill?"

I was troubled over the length of time it took Dr. Alvarez's staff to locate a lab that could do this different kind of test, making calls all over the country. I was in his office a total of three and a half hours, watching this nurse search in what looked like a little catalog. She changed her mind maybe ten times. She asked several people how much acid to put in, but nobody seemed to know what was going on. Finally, she settled all the details and told me to keep the urine on ice and bring it back. Hooty thought it was funny I had to keep his beer cooler in the bathtub and close the little container up extra careful every time.

By now, it was close to Christmas, and I waited ever day for a week to hear from the test. After a week I started calling the office. Naturally, they had one of them little "trees" I hate: If you're dying, press 1, if you need an appointment, press 2, if you need lab results, press 3, etc. Then the lab would come on and give you a bunch of choices. I was usually pretty tired of that by the time I got to my choice, so I'd say, "This is Thelma Sims and I wanna know what's going on with my lab test. Call this number."

By the end of the 3rd week, when Hooty took to calling, he wouldn't use that tree. He'd just punch 0 without listening to them choices and say, "Let me speak to that boy in the lab."

The boy finally agreed to call the Mayo clinic where they'd sent the test. The next day, the whole office just disappeared over the telephone. The fools took a whole week off for Christmas without warning us.

The first day they opened, me and Hooty was waitin' for 'em. "We don't want to be put off no more," I told the girl at the desk who looked like she might faint when she saw Hooty's mean look and the little strip of leather from the holster that he flashed when he opened his jacket. He give her that look where his eyes look like pieces of coal just about to flame up, that lump in his throat moving all around. The way he'd started balding and then let that bottom hair grow long made him look like some kinda outlaw, but it was that far away look in them eyes that made folks nervous.

Hooty told the receptionist we wanted to see that lab boy. Her lips trembled when she said, "I'll see." But she was back in a minute with him. Hooty had on his boots that make him almost as tall as me, but still about half as big around. It felt like he was standing on his tiptoes.

The downtown lab boy looked kinda like Hollywood: tall, dark and handsome. He wasn't prissy like the other boy, but he didn't look like much of a fighter either. He looked scared when he saw how mad Hooty was. Usually Hooty just grinned at everything, but he was hot now. The boy promised to call us later in the day, but it was a whole bloomin' week before we actually talked to a human instead of a recording again. On Friday morning, the boy called and said that the urine sample had never left Birmingham. I said, "Why on earth did they do that? Was they keeping it for theirselves for a little Christmas present?"

He said, real sheepishly, "They said they didn't know what to do with it." He added half-heartedly, "It is a real unusual test. Dr. Alvarez is the only one here who ever heard of it."

"Son," I said slyly, "let's get this down in writin', ever' name and ever detail just as clear as we can because I just might let a lawyer friend of mine take a look at it."

He sounded real nervous then, but he wrote it all out and

had it ready for me the next day when I came back with the third collection of my urine. I had got to be pretty expert by then. I prob'ly could've used one of them urinals by that time. The boy guaranteed me this specimen would get to the Mayo Clinic.

I got real busy workin' in the yard then. I had some fruit trees to fertilize, and I had the pine bark I'd been getting a little along at Walmart piled up behind the trailer. We had some good weather for about a week and I stayed busy every afternoon. See we have the front lot, and we have appearances to keep up. When my cousin Robert first rented that spot to us at Riff Raft Acres, he told me that being along the highway wouldn't be too bad. He showed me how we could build us a little deck at the back where we could see down to the water. That sunset on the water was mighty important to me, but the lots right on the water was way too expensive, and Robert wanted somebody on the front who'd keep up the yard and everything.

One morning out at the nursing home, I saw Dr. Meriweather. He'd been my doctor for years and years before he retired. Though he was nearly old enough to be a patient himself, he came out and visited some of the old folks every now and then out of the goodness of his heart. I cornered him in the coffee room and started pumping him for information.

"Dr. Meriweather," I began, "did you ever have a patient with a carcinoid tumor?"

He scratched his head and his eyes rolled up like they were trying to remember. "That's a pretty unusual ailment, Thelma, and I don't think I ever had the honor."

"They tell me they're not malignant," I said, "but I thought carcinoid meant cancer. You ever hear of a cancer that wasn't malignant?" I asked.

"Best I can remember those little buggers are hard to track down, real slow growers, but always malignant." Then he stopped and looked at me sideways, "You goin to medical school, Thelma, or you worrying about this for a reason?"

"I might be," I said, not answering either way.

He motioned for me to sit down and fixed me a cup of coffee. He always was the sweetest thing on earth. So I told him about the crazy things that had been happening.

"Thank God I'm beyond it," he said. "When I practiced medicine we didn't have all these wonders of modern science, but we could take the time to tell a patient what she needs to know."

Before I knew it, he was drawing those little pictures on a napkin like he used to in his office on the back of prescription pads. We talked awhile, and then he was scooting his chair back and standing up to go, saying "I tell you what you could do. You can make Robert get on the Internet and find all kinds of information, keep you just as up-to-date as any of the doctors nowadays. His boy's always carrying on through the e-mail with my grandson who can find me anything I want to ·

know about a whole bunch of subjects, some of which I can't discuss with a lady.

"You stay after it, Thelma, make 'em give you satisfaction. It's such a rat race today it's not even like the same profession. I'm surprised the patients don't start a revolution."

Then I started calling everyday again to see about the test, and finally I got a nurse who told me that the Mayo clinic said it could take anywhere from 1 to 3 months to get the test done. I just busted into tears right in the middle of her talking. I said, my voice just screaming, crazy sounding, like somebody else talking, "Them carcinoids are always cancer and cancer is always malignant. There ain't no such thing as benign cancer."

"Yes, m'am," she said, "I'm just relaying the message I was given. Dr. Alvarez thought you'd want to know." I told her I figured that fool Mexican just had a language problem. He ought to learn to speak English, that's what. She just got real quiet. I said, "I know it ain't your fault, it's just that I feel like beating the crap outta somebody, and I can't figure out who."

"Yes, m'am," she answered.

That's when I started calling the Cancer Society. Once I got them nice ladies on the phone who didn't treat me like a fool and I read all that stuff they mailed me, I felt like I was getting somewhere. I could at least figure out some things I didn't have to worry about. That's what gave me the confidence to ask Robert about the computer. He said Dwayne C., his boy, was the expert, but he couldn't use it these days because he'd been grounded.

Robert scratched his head and tugged on his T shirt that wasn't quite covering his belly, "Tell you the truth. It would save me a lot of grief if we could just move it up to your place for awhile."

"No, sir, I'm not letting you—" I started.

He wouldn't hear of it though, seemed too eager to get rid of it. By late afternoon Robert had showed me how to use it, set it up for me and all. He told me, when I tried to thank him, "Us riff raff has to stick together, hang on to the same raft." Then he gave me one his bear hugs and shuffled barefoot back down to his boat that he was always fixing.

Truth was his wife was the wickedest, fattest stepmother I ever seen, made him take that computer away from his boy cause she thought all that stuff he read on there would turn him into a gang member. She'd been looking over his shoulder watching him on those chat groups, saying they was ruining the English language, talking like colored folks, all that. Me and Hooty just started lettin' Dwayne C. come over here after school and use the thing all he wanted to till they got home from their jobs. Tickled us really.

Hooty even got us on America Online after I seen him in there with Dwayne C. giggling over them naked lady pictures on them chat groups. Besides they had a free 30-day trial thing I could use. Dwayne C. told Hooty the only gangs he was study-ing was gang banging. They laughed like two children, and only one of 'em s'pose to be one.

I started using everything I could to find out for myself. I started going to the computer every morning. I couldn't believe how much stuff you could learn about cancer just pushing them buttons. Some of it was written for them little medical students. I could tell by the way they made it sound so hard and used big words and long sentences you'd have read 10 times before you knew for sure it didn't make a bit of sense. But some of it was written just for patients, put out by the Cancer Society. Tell you the truth, I was about ready to open a practice. Hooty said, "Hell, you could do a whole lot better than them guys you paying a fortune to for nothing."

It seemed like doing my investigation kinda took my mind off the worry. It also helped me quit worrying so much to realize that even the experts don't always agree on stuff. Hooty didn't have any use for reading though and he just got madder. I started going online some at night while Hooty tuned into a baseball game in front of that television.

What I liked the most was the cancer chat group. One night I got up my nerve to try to talk on that thing since these little boxes would flash on automatically. I think they were trying to sell memberships or something. These kids would all be talking about how much they drank, how much they liked sex, stuff like that. I liked listening in, kinda like when I was a girl and Mama 'n' em would listen in on the party line. I never did that though. It seemed wrong to me.

This was different. The people wanted you to listen. They had funny names like *Surfer* and *Sexad* and *GVMESMHD*. They'd say stuff like:

ssssup?

So how old is everybody in here?

They didn't want to tell how old they were; all of 'em wanted to be older than they were. One guy said, "I'm sure I'm the oldest person in the room; I'm 26."

So I just spoke up and I told 'em I was exactly twice his age—52, and he said, "No come on, I'm serious." They couldn't believe there was anybody that old. I loosened up a little, but I didn't say much for awhile. Then I asked casually, "Anybody in here can tell me how to get to the cancer chat group?" I was amazed at how hard that was to ask. My palms were sweaty and my throat felt tight, like I needed to clear it but I couldn't.

It was a minute before somebody told me what keyword to use and how to try it. Then four or five of the kids said stuff like:

"Hang in there."

"I hope you find it."

But by the time I left the "room," they were already back to praising Jack Daniel and talking about how big their bosoms were.

The talk on the cancer chat was different. There would still be two or three conversations going at once, but people would be talking about how long they'd been in chemo, how long it took their hair to grow back, stuff like that. One lady was about to scream because she had gone in for chemo and they put the wrong stuff in her veins. Several people suggested she shoot something poisonous in the veins of some lab technicians. That seemed like a pretty good idea to me, too. Then some guy came on the screen, saying, "Ooooooooooooooooooo, help me I am dying of cancer."

A lady named *ur4given* answered, "We're right here, how can we help." But the guy never said anything else, and most folks figured he was a fake. I didn't know what to think, but it gave me the creeps. I just signed off then and went to bed, but I couldn't get that scream, that "Ooooooooooooooooooooo" out of my mind. I also thought horrible things about kidnapping that lab boy and torturing him. Or maybe the makeup queen to scrub her for about an hour. I decided all this stuff could make you crazy if you let it. Maybe Dwayne C. *was* being corrupted by that computer. It was worse than the television to give you crazy ideas because all those people were going through real life. I couldn't let go of the idea that the lady who had the wrong chemicals put in her veins ought to poison some lab technicians. I didn't sleep much at all anymore.

One morning I stared at myself in the mirror after breakfast. I used to pull my hair back in a tight bun every morning, but lately I had just let it straggle, especially since I had to keep putting my hat on and off. Them eyes looking back at me from under that hot blue hat were almost purple, little amethysts stuck in the dough of my face. I had lost a lot of weight since all this stuff had started and my neck showed it, all gobbled and flabby at the throat.

I didn't like what I saw. I got the scissors and cut my hair off real short like a boy's. Then I got in the tub and soaked myself for over an hour. I put on lots of perfume and some dangling earbobs since my hair was so short it looked like something was missing. When Hooty woke up, he asked me if I had a boyfriend or something. I told him, "Yeah, Dr. Alvarez."

"You mess with that fool and I'll fix him," Hooty said, and that dark cloud came over his face. It seemed like he just couldn't let go of worrying over me. Hooty just went to work at the plastic factory and came home and drank beer in front of the TV. One night he came in with two Atlanta Braves hats and told me he thought maybe I'd like a new hat to go with my new image. I tried wearing it some, but I still liked my Paris blue one best. Hooty never wore his cap outside the house, but he'd put it on every night when whatever game he was watching came on.

Usually on Saturday mornings before the ball games on television started, Hooty would watch Robert make bullets. In his basement, Robert had a machine where he made his own bullets, hollow points he called them. I never paid them any mind, couldn't stand the sound of a gun. When Hooty insisted I learn how to fire one, I snapped at him, "Why do I need to learn if I'm gonna sleep with the best crack shot in the county and my cousin's always down there in his own private arsenal?"

One Saturday in the spring just when the buds on the trees had started to bust open and make those tiny little baby fists of leaves, I sat on the deck, sweat pouring from working some fertilizer in around my azaleas. I could hear Hooty and Robert off in the woods target shooting as I made my way to the mailbox.

That's the day the crazy mail came. There it was in the mail without any letter to explain to us or anything except we could see where Dr. Alvarez had written, "Mail to Ms. Sims." The lab report said: *Test canceled by Reference Laboratory. Above test requires that ph of specimen be between 1.0 and 5.0. Please resubmit if desired.*

I cried so hard when Hooty came in I couldn't talk, just handed him the letter. "Baby, we gonna get that sumbich," Hooty hissed, twirling that pistol. The finish on the barrel was polished so much it flashed in the sunlight like a thunderbolt.

"Now, Hooty, don't start talking like that," I tried to say, but he wasn't about to stop. I still can't believe I let him talk me into it.

Hooty jumped the switch and made the old Chevy run somehow. We put them baseball caps on backwards and cut the radio up loud.

We looked just like them gangs we'd heard about. We had even bought us some Afro-tique panty hose to put over our faces, so we'd look colored. We stalked that doctor like we'd been doing it all our lives. We saw him come out of that Catholic church, looking all smug and satisfied. We followed him home and just as he got out of the car, we got a good look at him.

I could see his face as he squinted to see what an old car like ours was doing on a hifalutin' street like his. I saw his face change when he saw the gun, his mouth fall open. His little bug eyes looked like they might pop open. I had to work hard to keep my eyes on the road, drive that car as fast as I could. Hooty fired the pistol. Bull's eye: right between the legs! Blood spurted everywhere as Alvarez fell to the ground, reaching out as if he thought we would stop and help him. Then I gunned the motor and we were out of that little cul de sac before anybody could have seen us.

We laughed till we cried. "Let that fool see what it's like to be a victim of the medical profession," Hooty said.

"Wonder if they'll be able to find him a receptacle to pee in now," I answered in a high-pitched voice that didn't sound like mine. We dumped that old car at the bottom of the heap in my uncle's scrap yard like we'd been doing that kind of stuff every Sunday.

I'm not saying we were right, but I am telling you we felt the sweet taste of revenge, riding home with the smell of fresh rain around us. I might be dying and I might not, but I ain't going back to no doctors, and I won't have to die without knowing the satisfaction of revenge. All I had to do to get up my nerve was close my eyes and remember that woman who had the wrong stuff put in her veins or that scream, "ooooooooooooooooooh I am dying."

They tell me holding grudges will cause cancer. You have to do something about stuff that makes you angry. They have documented cases of people who "deal with their anger" and make their tumors disappear.

When we went to bed that night, Hooty took me in his arms, and it was kinda like coming home after a long time away.

"You know what?" I said, just as he was dozing off. "I just might take that GED class at the library and become a LPN."

Hooty never answered, but I knew he heard me. Somehow I also knew I'd be able to count on him to see me through.

THINGS VISIBLE AND INVISIBLE

Damrell imagines herself on a plush Persian carpet, flying without the airplane—self-sufficient, peaceful. Grateful for the two-seater, she glances at the stranger sleeping beside her. She looks through the narrow window at the bed of fluffy pink clouds, the stuff of sunsets somewhere between Detroit and New York. From her home in Memphis, she has flown to Denver via St. Paul often, but going to the Big Apple via Detroit is new. She likes the energy of the Detroit passengers when they board. Like Act II, she thinks.

She remembers using the magic carpet in creative visualizations class after her mastectomy, during chemo, how foolish she felt at first. She decides her carpet *is* magical: within minutes of the sunset, she witnesses the moon, full and clear—its light not blinding like the sun. She, who once had all the answers, gazes into the face of the moon, longing for illumination. She avoids her reflection in the small, oval window, eyes downcast. With ambivalence, she anticipates the reunion with her cousin who is like a sister. Their complex rivalry runs as deep as their affection. Karma is the zany cousin who had sense enough to leave.

Behind Damrell, a curvaceous musician chatters with a man twice her age. At first Damrell's annoyed, but they're interesting. She enjoys eavesdropping. It demands so little.

"Yeah, I own a little restaurant on the upper East Side," the older guy says, his pronunciation defining him as a New Yorker. "Best food in New York. We feature the Southern cuisine, you know. Doing very well. Very well. We had the legendary

Catherine DeNeuve in the other night, and she loved it. I had to check her out to be sure when I heard who she was. I mean, she must be 60, but I swear she looked 30."

Damrell thinks of *Les Liasons Dangereuse,* a movie she watched as a graduate student in New England years ago. She remembers how delicate, how fragile DeNeuve's blonde beauty was. She wished then she looked like the actress; she wishes it more now as she runs her long slender hand across the soft, downy stubble that covers her scalp. She fingers the heavy gold earrings Geoff gave her last month, wondering if he thought of them himself. Probably purchased by his pert, young nurse who is more likely to know how a large pair of classy earrings can detract from "the sheared look."

"So is Detroit as bad as it sounds?" the older man asks. Damrell smiles, jots in her travel journal, *He's so like a New Yorker, unfamiliar with anything west of the Hudson River.*

The girl answers in her soft, mellow voice, "I like Detroit, actually. I mean we have a lot of crime. I had a friend in high school who was gunned down. That was pretty rough, you know? But in my part of the city, we have the second lowest crime rate of any neighborhood its size in the country. So you just have to figure ways to look at things. And I love the music scene. Detroit has great sound."

"Yeah, that's true. You can't always go by what you hear, you know?" the New Yorker says. Damrell softens toward the man when she hears him say he had to leave town, get away to San Diego to visit friends because his mother's sick, "very sick, having trouble with the radiation, ya know? My sister was very angry that I left. But you gotta deal with these things the way you gotta, you know?"

Damrell knows his reasoning well. The young woman consoles the chatty passenger with unusual maturity. Damrell had noticed her soft eyes and wild curls when she gently laid her guitar case in the overhead bin. Just when she decides the girl looks like Jesus with a perm, Damrell hears her say, "I'm on my way to Europe, to the Holy Land to direct music for a group of pilgrims. You know, it'll be so neat to walk on trails where Jesus walked, see the things He saw."

The older guy says, "Yeah."

Within half an hour, the guy has made a successful move on the girl. Damrell hears smacking noises, takes out her compact to be sure she's not imagining such sleazy behavior. She isn't. The girl has raised the arm rest between them and covered herself with a blanket. She may even be the aggressor. Damrell's initial response is anger. Nobody has manners any more! She closes her eyes though and allows herself to feel the wicked flame that grows inside her as she hears them breathe heavily. Then she contents herself flipping through *Architectural Digest* after throwing *Vogue,* with its eternal plunging necklines, back to the flight attendant as if it were a hot potato.

She sees an antebellum home, recently restored, near Atlanta, skims the architect's comments. The wide porch reminds her of her grandmother's home where she and Geoff doubledated with Karma and her endless suitors. They threw weekend parties there that Damrell was sure made her grandmother scream in her coffin. The house, which had been unoccupied since they were in high school, provided the perfect escape since it was only 30 miles from Memphis.

Karma prided herself on having sex with a different guy in every bedroom as often as possible. She was like a wild, exotic animal, wearing her leopard or tiger scarves—untamed green eyes seductive over the sheer fabric at her slender neck.

Damrell and Geoff were not wild, but they had enjoyed the excitement of Karma's crazy behavior. In the feather bed where her grandparents had lain under the musty quilts Geoff, enticed by Karma's moans in the next room, reached toward Damrell with an urgency unknown to them now. Geoff was compact, a small man with no trace of fat on his warm, youthful body.

Geoff is still lean, muscular in his forties. He still turns to her in the night, though not as often now. He has put his energy into his work, is consumed by it. A driven man, he often sleeps at the hospital where he consults with radiologists and anesthesiologists at dawn before going to surgery.

Damrell's heart races with her first glimpse of the city's lights. The bridges gleam like emerald necklaces, the clusters of light like sparkling diamonds. Something vital in her clicks on, as if she's seen an old lover. Or the ghost of Geoff on their first trip to the city. She strains to see more from the small window. She quickens, recognizing familiar sights that spark memories drenched in pleasure.

The young man next to her stretches awake. Under his bristly moustache, full lips smile at her. She is certain he has overheard the couple. She colors at the intimacy of seeing him awaken, buttoning the wrinkled shirt that covers his hairy chest and re-knotting his tie which is patterned with Matisse-like swirls of tangerine and deep green against a sea of aquamarine.

"Why are you coming to the Big Apple?" he asks, his gentle grey eyes scanning her breasts.

"Family visit. You?" she answers softly, turning toward him.

"I'm an artist from Arizona, in town to do some work with my agent." He is confident, but tentative, tells her about the fiancée he dropped because he must have his independence as an artist.

"I swear my husband would be relieved if I died," she exaggerates. "He loves me, but he loves his work more." As soon as she tosses off phrases like *if I died* casually, she wants to bite her tongue. *To die for, wish I were dead, she's killing herself, I 'bout died* . . . over and over those deadly phrases invade her. She realizes the artist is waiting for her to continue. "I . . . I . . . mean, he's a surgeon."

The artist says in a soft voice, "Say no more; my dad's a surgeon. Here's my card. I show my work at the Grand Central Gallery, watch for it, ok? Come by some time."

"Sure," she says, amazed that the small gift of the card burns with significance. Tears spring to her eyes. She fumbles in her purse, rips out a deposit slip from her checkbook and gives him her address.

"Damrell?" he puzzles.

"It's a family name, a Southern thing." She smiles, placing his card in her organizer. Then he's gone, squeezing into the mob of hurried passengers in the aisle.

Impulsively, she asks the heavy man behind her for his card, too, when they are jammed together in the aisle, waiting to deplane. "I'm visiting someone from Georgia; we may just have to check out your authenticity with the Southern cuisine."

"Love to have you," he beams.

"By the way," she says, her voice more intimate than she means it to be, "I'm running away from radiation, too. Sometimes we just have to. Good luck."

She makes her way down the aisle and into the vast space at Kennedy airport. She books flights through La Guardia, but Geoff's secretary made these plans. She follows the herd of people from her plane. They all seem to know where they're going, but she watches carefully for the Domestic Baggage signs. Suddenly, the other passengers disappear as she fits her carry-on suitcase above the pull-cart.

At the information desk a black woman, wearing gold hoop earrings and a sapphire in her nose, smiles warmly and says in an accent Damrell pegs as British, "Follow me. You're almost there; you only missed one turn."

Damrell spots her heavy bags, finds the strength to yank them off the belt quickly the way people in this city do. She even walks faster though she's in no hurry.

She feasts on people-watching. In elementary school, her classmates were just biding time while geography was taught but she was enthralled, loved the different customs, different diets.

A veiled woman in a sheer skirt and a Spanish woman in high heels wearing a cheap red dress both clutch children whose eyes are big with wonder. Mothers from Egypt, from Rio de Janiero, from Pakistan murmur to their children in that universal language of maternal love. Damrell hears more foreign tongues than native. She loves this world fusion, this shrinking globe that Geoff and his friends curse along with every move the Federal "gov'ment" makes.

Finding her way to the taxi stand is hectic. Damrell pushes the heavy suitcases and her computer around the maze. She calls Karma, her cousin, but she gets only a New York voice on the machine. No way there could be two Karma Stephens even in Manhattan. Damrell's face is flushed, the cashmere sweater airplane-damp. In the narrow toilet stall, she changes into a silk blouse. She'll need the sweater when the flash passes, so she ties it to the strap on her carry-on. Cooler, she glances in the bar for the man from Arizona, but he isn't there, of course.

An older man, tall and handsome, in a black fur-trimmed topcoat gazes at her. She feels slightly lifted by his attention. The man at the taxi stand frowns when she allows the woman behind her, with three small children, to go ahead. When she tries to explain, the oily man looks down at her, his nose tilted in condescension, and cuts her off, "Where to, lady? Let's keep it moving!"

Damrell exhales a sigh, makes a point of staring at his nostril hairs which need trimming. It's New York, she thinks. No place like it. Her notion is quickly confirmed when she plops in the back seat of a taxi driven by a man of indeterminate race whom she asks, "May I roll the window down?"

His dark, thick brows disappear in the curly hairline, as if she's speaking Martian. "Yeah," he says, baffled by manners. His eyebrow arches when she gives him the specific directions Karma suggested.

"I want to go up West Side Highway to Riverside Drive at

110th Street." She wonders whether he objects to her directions or to her presence in the universe. Karma had told her to avoid turbaned cabbies, claiming they hate American women. Like she had a choice. He pulls up across the street from the apartment and pops the trunk open.

"I'll need you to lift my suitcase out of the trunk," she says. He offers no comment, but sticks his hand out at the window separating them, weary disgust twisting his mouth.

"I need a receipt, please," she says.

He holds his hand out. Finally he says "For how much?"

"Nineteen dollars," she says, noting that the bill is $18.60, "and I'll need you to lift my suitcase out of the trunk." She holds her breath, sure he'll murder her for tipping him an insulting 40 cents. He doesn't, but he jerks her luggage out of the taxi and throws it toward her. She gives him her best Southern belle smile, then makes her way slowly across the street. Heavy-laden, Damrell retreats into the cloister of the lobby and the safety of the doorman's protection.

Karma is almost as tall as the hand-carved, mahogany armoire where she hangs Damrell's coat. Her chic, thin body in black silk slacks tucked in suede ankle boots, towers over Damrell, seated on their grandmother's love seat. In no time, Karma has ruled out all Damrell's suggestions for the weekend: the opera, the dance concert and the down-home dinner on the East side. "Who the hell's Catherine DeNeuve?" Karma asks, rumpling her boyish crew cut.

Damrell smiles, "Never mind. What's with the cigarette holder?"

Karma tries to brush it off, "I've always used one. Let's go see *Vagina Dialogues,* ok*?"*

Damrell doesn't remember Karma smoking period. "I really want to see *The Music Man*," Damrell insists, "I promised Geoff. The girl who sings the lead was one of his patients. He'll pay for the tickets." Damrell wants good seats, but they hurry instead to the two-fers line and wind up with separate seats in the balcony.

"Wasn't the librarian luminous when she sang 'Till There Was You,' just radiating light!" Damrell squeals when they find each other in the lobby.

"I hate musicals," Karma sighs, exaggerating boredom. "Ever since I took that acting class down in the Village, I've preferred off-Broadway. Which reminds me of a perfect bar I want to take you to where some of the actors hang out, ok?"

Damrell is surprised Karma goes through the charade of asking. At Cafe des Acteurs, Damrell downs her first drink quickly and jabs her cousin, "Looks like you could support the playwright and buy a decent seat since you're so artsy, even taking acting lessons. Like you need 'em; you've been acting all your life."

"Miz Melanie, the bourgeois cousin from the provinces," Karma quips, grinning slyly, more interested in taking inventory of available men. The soft-spoken Cuban waiter knows Karma, treats her like a regular, often flashing a Desi Arnez smile toward her. The elegant man next to them drinks three martinis before Damrell finishes her second Manhattan. He sloshes Bombay gin on his navy silk suit, a wool scarf the color of sand thrown across his shoulder—"dashing" her mother would call him. His tall, blond looks intrigue Damrell; she admires his chiseled facial features, discounts his thin frame. Damrell decides he looks German: his long nose tilted under cold blue eyes. His military air is attractive initially, but it disintegrates with each swish of the martini glass.

He insists on buying their drinks, then on giving them a ride home. "I have a driver," he slurs.

Damrell, assuming it's out of the question, snaps, "So what!" However, she sees from Karma's impish eyes, fixed on the stranger's, that her cousin intends to take him up on the offer. The alcohol has loosened Damrell's reserve—why expect Karma to have any limits?

"You both look like Shirley MacLaine. Are you sisters? Wouldn't that be fun!" he mumbles to Karma. "I wanna turn you over."

The waiter has not been as friendly since the man took over, but Damrell glances toward him. As she pulls on her jacket she whispers, "Will we be safe with this guy?" He nods a hesitant yes. She wonders what the stranger means about turning Karma over . . . spanking? This was not the fling Damrell had in mind. Monogamy seems irresistible at the moment.

The man has his driver pour him another martini from the bar in the limo before they leave the parking area. "Fix you ladies anything?" the driver asks in a gentle voice that reassures Damrell, his kinky silver temples gleaming against dark skin. As the limo races up Broadway, Damrell prays they arrive home intact. She sees an envelope on the floor, a formal invitation in small calligraphy. "Excuse me," she says, tapping the silk sleeve thrown across the seat, and hands the card to the stranger. As if she flipped a switch, he instantly turns sadistic,

"You trollop! Don't pry into my affairs. Who do you think you are? I'll give you something to snoop about!"

"Hey come on, man, chill out," Karma says, which snaps him out of the tantrum momentarily. She whispers seductively, "What you need is some dancin', a little shakin' down. We could fix you up, sweetheart." She leans toward him, revealing her flat, boyish breasts. Damrell winces. Karma tells the driver, pointing boldly, "Take us to some good jazz up in Harlem. Let's have some action." This is a side of her cousin Damrell hasn't seen before. Damrell doesn't like it, but she's afraid to speak even before the man's blue eyes glare at them, raging in response to Karma's offer.

"You stupid bitches, you're trying to take me to a faggot dive."

The driver speaks to him in a soothing tone, "Take it easy now, man."

He yells louder, "Faster, drive 'em crazy, let's give them something they won't forget." When the driver floorboards it, the glasses in the bar tinkle as if to warn them of a crash. At the first traffic light, the car screeches to a halt, throwing one glass to the floor where it rolls around with a life of its own. Otherwise, a surreal quiet looms inside the sleek, black vehicle. Karma has pulled a leather poncho over her head as if she's hiding.

Damrell feels a giddy giggle rising in her throat, which she suppresses. She knows her brain is soaked, but she doesn't want her panties soaked, too. Damrell's giddiness teetering toward hysteria, she whispers to Karma who doesn't answer, "Lawsy, Miz Scarlet, I got to pee pee." Her cousin remains silent under the hood. The only sound is the swish of tires racing against wet pavement.

The black man chuckles softly, his eyes smiling at Damrell from the rearview mirror, but the blond man goes berserk again. "Faster, faster," he commands the driver who doesn't obey this time. "You shabby, racist bitches, coming up here, feeding off the fat of our land . . . " he begins a tirade that is cut short by the squeal of brakes outside Karma's building.

They are out of the car quickly, before the maniac can focus his eyes or figure what's happening. Karma is all giggles now, a shrill laughter like a hyena trapped in a maze of concrete and asphalt--lonely, out of place. Damrell impulsively hugs the black man who is soft like a teddy bear. "I can't believe we made it home," she whispers.

He shakes his head with a weary smile, "I've seen it all, honey chile. Seen it all."

"That bastard's crazy as hell," Karma adds as if she's telling the creased, mahogany face something he hasn't figured out.

All three realize at the same time the wild one has heard Karma. The glazed blue eyes widen as the window lowers and the man inside the limo yells, "Don't screw around with me, you filthy gold-digging dikes!"

Damrell, emboldened by the booze and the proximity of the doorman, yells back at him, "No, *you* don't screw *us*! That's your problem." Eyes bulging as if they might explode, his mouth gapes in shock. Her sudden switch from the demure cousin has confused him. Her heart races—exhilaration, adrenaline pumping in her veins. "I was kind to you when you were a boring, pathetic drunk nobody else would talk to." She sticks her face inside the window, "I was kind to you. You see this face? This is the face of kindness. Don't you ever forget it."

She's still pointing to the face when he jumps out of the car and staggers after them, his overcoat dripping.

"Don't try to pull that crap with me," he demands hoarsely.

"Get over it," Karma says over her shoulder, laughing already, only an arm's length from the doorman and the safety of a locked door. Suddenly, Karma bends over, slips the silk slacks down far enough to moon him and screams, "Pervert!" Laughing hysterically, Damrell rushes into the cold, marble lobby.

Dusting lint from his epaulets, the doorman stares straight ahead like a Beefeater at the Tower of London. He avoids Damrell's gaping mouth, her widened hazel eyes when she sees Karma slap, then kiss, the stranger hungrily, his long-fingered hands digging into her shapely derriere. He shoves her against the brownstone, jerking her blouse open and stumbling on her feet. Karma's face is aglow, like fire.

Damrell's face flushes as she digs in her purse for the key. She escapes into the elevator, glad to disappear into the quiet privacy. Damrell staggers into the dark room, takes off her clothes and has just buttoned the green satin pajama top when she hears them crash into the door, shattering her asylum.

"Bengt here has to use the john," Karma slurs as she leads the pale-faced man down the hallway. Karma throws a set of satin leopard-skin sheets toward the sofa, then rushes back to the bathroom where the sound of vomit competes with its odor—putrid, ruined.

Damrell crawls into the sheets, feigns sleep when she hears

Karma brew an almond-scented coffee whose aroma fills the room. It seems like hours that she hears the soft murmurs and seductive laughter interspersed with moans and rhythmic squeaking of bedsprings. They might as well be teenagers again. Karma will never grow up, but what a way to go, Damrell thinks as she hears her cousin calling out to God, screeching with intensity. Enflamed by the noisy lovemaking, Damrell recalls the stranger coming on to her first. She had enjoyed the attention, the stirring she felt when he'd brushed against her thigh. She imagines the young artist, how gentle he'd have been with her. He would have loosened her blouse and gently kissed her scar, her badge. She feels the tears coming, but she blocks them. There is someone in the room with her! She is certain.

Then she hears the low, guttural laughter as the stark white sheet moves toward her. "Good God, Karma! What are you doing?"

The man's voice answers in an attempt to sound Southern, "We thought ya'll might be missing the Klan!"

Karma jerks the sheet off and crawls in bed with Damrell. "Bengt here is gonna fix us an omelet, while we snuggle and listen to his corny jokes."

"That's not funny," he chuckles. He wraps his sheet around pale blue bikini briefs, the same color as his eyes. Damrell readily accepts the Bloody Mary he brings her.

"It's still night time," she says.

"That's ok. What the hell," he mutters, headed back to the smell of scorching butter.

"The man is a beast." Karma smiles, her full lips relaxed around the pearly teeth. She lights a cigarette, offers Damrell one.

"No, thanks," Damrell snaps. "Aren't you cold?" She has just realized Karma is stark naked.

"Are you kidding, with Bengt, the star of Swedish porn here?" Her small breasts jiggle as she laughs and arches her back as if to display her own acrobatic skill. Damrell is stunned by the tears that spring to her eyes when she feels the stirring in her belly, a confusing mixture of envy, resentment, and stimulation.

"I'll have another Bloody Mary," Damrell yells to Bengt. She tastes the vodka, knows it's strong, wants it to be.

Karma lights candles all around the room before Bengt brings them breakfast in bed. The girls tell stories about their adolescent escapades, which of course turn to sex. Bengt glances too often at Damrell's long, shapely legs in the satin boxers. She crawls under the cover, but she keeps talking, "Most of Karma's suitors started out with me. She stole all my boyfriends."

"Old Bengt here drinks vodka straight. He has a hollow leg," Karma quips.

"Three," he smiles.

Damrell sees the bulge in his briefs. His eyes tell her he saw the glimpse. "Tell us about your youth in Sweden," she says. In the fog of dawn, she knows it's going to happen. Bengt's head rests in Karma's lap, his hand is silky against Damrell's thigh. "What the hell. We'll never get to sleep unless we do this," Damrell whispers.

His forbidden touch electrifies her, fills her with memories of hot summer nights double-dating with Karma and who-

ever. Damrell and Geoff would be "smooching in moderation,"
as he calls it now, teasing her. Back then, Karma's moans and
labored breathing had tantalized her. She wants to feel that
way again: alive, fresh, new.

When Bengt penetrates her awkward shyness, she soars
into the lightning that Karma knows. It's quick, impersonal
and strangely satisfying. Damrell is still breathing heavily when
she hears them tiptoe out with their sheets overhead again.
"OOOOOOOO," Karma giggles, "I am the ghost of Christmas
yet to come."

In no time, she hears the slap against flesh and Karma's
squeals and moans again. "Such a naughty girl," one of them
mimics parentally. She can't even tell which. She doesn't care.
She wants to go home.

Damrell calls Geoff. His voice is warm, like molasses in her
ear, "I'm glad you're having fun."

"You're not so boring after all. Maybe it isn't a fling I need,
but you," she blurts, then howls with laughter.

"What?" his startled, still groggy voice asks. "Babeeeee? Have
you and Karma been drinking?"

"I love you, boy," she whispers and slips the phone into its
cradle.

She covers her mangled breast with the sheet, closes her
scratchy eyes and tries to calm down. Bengt hadn't noticed
she never took her top off. Of course, she embraces the knowledge that it hadn't mattered to either of them, but Damrell
also mourns the lost fantasy of the artist's soft kiss. She wants
the mastectomy to matter and not matter at the same time.
Outside, the fire escape flickers with shadows too close to

the giant windows. She shivers, then sobs softly into the scented sheet, its softness enveloping her.

Next morning, she awakens to a powdery snowfall in Riverside Park, sparkling in the morning sun outside the window. It reminds her of the elves who used to sled through sugary snow on the flickering, grey television screen of her youth. She hears the jingle, "Godchaux Sugar!"

Damrell's temple aches just above the ear. She touches her thin hair to be sure someone has not cut a stripe along her skull. She makes a toga of the sheet, sits in the windowsill and eats vanilla ice-cream, from the carton. Damrell explains to Karma when she appears, puffy-eyed and sheepish, "It was the only thing in the fridge. Tallulah once said ice cream makes a good hangover cure."

Karma yawns and shimmies, "To shake the ache," she mutters, never noticing that Damrell pulls the sheet tighter or that the park is covered with the wondrous white that had thrilled them as innocent girls so many years ago.

BELLE'S BALLS

Belle Henderson had raised more money for the Fine Arts Forum than any previous hostess when she coordinated its annual masquerade ball last Halloween. She was also known throughout the state for her annual homecoming ball at Vinemont College. Silently congratulating herself for one of many thankless duties as the president's wife, she glanced back at the tables she'd centered with the school's colors: metallic gold gift bags anchored by purple balloons.

Belle bounded up the red velvet stairs for her afternoon workout. Catching a glimpse of herself in the mirror, she un-snapped the red athletic bra. Belle knew she looked great in mid-life. She had the body of a dancer—leggy, muscular . . . ready.

During Chet's moodiness following a showdown with the Faculty Senate, he had said, running freckled fingers through his pale, thinning hair, "Young George Armand seems to take a fancy to you, dear. Perhaps you could get through to him."

That's how it started, innocently enough, but the plan had backfired on Belle. She was determined not to be a notch on Armand's jockstrap, but she thought of him far too often. She grimaced over the irony that recollections of Armand with his perfect buns and smoldering eyes had led to her initial discovery of exercise as a physical outlet.

Belle often worked out after feeling aroused by Armand, who had complained about her decorating budget when she had the gym installed. She now was led to the treadmill by anger toward him and his nosy faculty friends out to get her husband fired. Sexual energy, poisonous anger, whatever—she loved a good workout. She moved smoothly on the Nordic Trak, listening to jazz from the intercom. She loved the sight of her breasts moving to the rhythm of the sensual music.

She remembered the first time she had seen Armand at a reception after a board meeting. He hovered in the corner with a group of angry, bearded profs, his hands gesturing so passionately she thought he'd drop the cigarette he hungrily sucked. She figured if he made love with the intensity he smoked cigarettes, he could be deadly.

Her jogging speed increased, as her anger escalated. When she realized she was fantasizing about the S. O. B. again, she dismissed him. He was probably working through some lapsed Catholic guilt at her expense, flirting the way he did. To hell with him. Ironically, if it weren't for him, she might not have invested in her exercise equipment.

Belle would be damned if she'd allow these power games to destroy her. She broke a good sweat on the machine after half an hour, then cooled down on her favorite piece of equipment, a machine that stretched the neck and shoulders as well as the lower back.

Belle purged in the sauna. No way anybody could ever smother the spirit of Belle Henderson, she thought. Lying in the steam, Belle could escape hassles completely, steaming life's impurities out of her system. After much resistance, she had convinced Chet to install the sauna. The arched entranceway, decorated with exotic plants and rough woods made a striking contrast with what was otherwise a lifeless decor imposed upon them.

The young Turks on campus had, predictably, turned it into an issue. And now she had to entertain them, host yet another ball.

Sweat poured from her body now, the way she liked it. Deeply breathing, as she had learned from yoga, she held the air in her chest, watching her ample breasts rise with the effort. She knew her body and its power. The physical sweat of the sauna was better than sex, beyond it somehow, and so easy to arrange. Just turn the knob and lie back. *Oh, God, it's good*, she thought, raising her knees to do a few pelvic tilts for the lower back.

She conditioned her hair, oozed the gel into her thick silver hair. She laughed to think how easily she could seduce that self-righteous Armand if she decided to. Realizing she had at least a thousand things to do, she checked her list once more before she dressed.

The red convertible made its way toward the top of the mountain, the lights of the city twinkling like scattered jewels behind. Armand shifted gears as he took a curve, exulting in the way the car hugged the road. Intoxicated by the heavy scent of magnolias lining the drive, he smiled at the visiting playwright who eyed him sensually. Armand focused on the narrow brick road that led to the president's mansion. The fog turned to mist just as they reached the hill. Armand sang out, "Follow the yellow brick road."

His guest tried the updated version, "Git on down git on down de rohoad." When the Greek revival mansion came into view gleaming atop the hill Valentino gasped, "Far out." The aging playwright sucked on a joint, the youthful gesture defying his grey temples.

The home was, indeed, spectacular: sturdy white columns lined the front, the marble veranda glistening in the wet, dark night. A spiral staircase led to the graceful balcony off the bedroom on the second floor where literally hundreds of candles burned from the bathroom window. In the fog, the candlelight formed small halos that matched the glow from the pearly white globes lighting the path to the doorway.

"What light from yonder window glows?" the playwright chuckled.

"That blaze belongs to the first lady," George explained. "That's milady's royal health club I told you about. She's hot, on the prowl. You'll find Hogarth etchings if you look around— pornographic art at its finest right next to some fussy Victorian atrocity left by the last president's wife. Word has it Belle and some famous poet struck up such a steam one night they couldn't keep their hands off each other at the dinner table. That's when prominent guests quit staying overnight at the mansion."

Valentino, bored by such prattle, scoffed—swooping his cape like a vampire in the foggy light. He flicked a cigarette butt into the flower bed just before the door opened and Belle appeared in a soft red dress, the light behind her glowing. Her silver hair glistened, radiating more an aura than a sheen. George whispered, "I swear I see heat outlining her body by half an inch, man. Do you?"

The visitor responded, straining to focus, "Your brain's fried by the weed." They laughed as they approached her.

"Good evening," she said to Valentino, taking his hand in hers. "I've admired your work for years, saw your first play in Rome years ago." Her navy blue eyes were intense, electric. Her hands held the flattered dramatist's firmly. George, realizing that Valentino was no longer bored but captured, shrugged and headed for the bar.

A cluster of women eyed George. He smiled toward them, lifted his glass as if to flaunt his drinking, a man on the town. He joined them later on the sun porch, a small bevy buzzing with gossip. A thin woman with intense grey eyes asked, her husky voice coming from a cloud of smoke, "Is that to suggest she's a Southern belle or is that really her name?" Her white silk skirt swished above her athletic shoes. The bags under her eyes sagged like jaundiced bruises, the yellow puff rippled with faded lilac.

"She's the belle from hell! A helluva belle!" a woman with a voice like thick molasses joked.

Husky laughter followed another cloud of smoke. "Where is she from, really?" the thin woman wanted to know.

The curvaceous jokester, a red-head in her sixties—self-appointed historian—answered, "Florida. Most of us attribute Belle's behavior to her years at Columbia. As we say in the Delta, 'She's just nevah been the saaaaame.' Even lost her Southern accent. She's still the belle of the ball though, gives the best parties in town. By the way, Belle *is* her name."

When Armand joined the covey, the chemistry of the group changed: the thin husky woman lit a cigarette and walked away. The redhead, Belle's neighbor, squealed as she squeezed his hand hello, "Professor Armand, I've heard you're a mess."

From the sun porch, they saw the lights flicker as if they were at the theatre, an insistent signal that couldn't be ignored. Valentino's shrill voice carried, "A dramatic way to bring them to the table!" Then he leaned closer to Belle, and Armand heard him whisper, "Where *did* you get that enchanting dress?"

"Neiman Marcus," she drawled and swirled around, making the lace reveal new places. The neckline cut almost to her waist where her eyes lingered for a perfectly timed second before she turned her face up toward Valentino and extended her hand, which Valentino kissed, then led her to the table. The gesture gave her cheeks a rosy glow to match the dress. She placed Valentino in the seat of honor next to the president, herself directly across from him on Chet's deaf side. *Armand* (in perfect calligraphy) appeared on the place card next to the playwright.

Armand's drink, the only one brought to the table, sloshed when he took his seat. He looked sheepishly toward his hostess, but she ignored him. "I'm so glad you were able to join us for dinner before the ball," she said to Valentino. "There will be so many people here later. Women still love to dress up and dance no matter how much the younger set try to destroy the romance of formal dress. I get so perturbed about it, having traveled abroad enough to know how a woman should feel in an evening gown. I assure you it's a coup to get our faculty to dress formally." She slanted her eyes toward Armand.

The woman in silk laughed, a husky mystery surrounding her amusement. "I saw an article in the *Chronicle* the other day entitled "The F Word in Academia." She paused for the silence that fell, then added, "Fashion. It's imperative that we dress down unless we want to turn into administrators."

After an awkward halt, the conversation took on the boring drone of academia: stories about campus activities, talk of the city's expansion with its threat to the halls of ivy, etc. Normally there was a verbal fencing match wherein controversy was flirted with, hinted at, but never openly alluded to. It was a comfortable game, and everyone knew their roles, their boundaries. Tonight, Armand felt stifled by borders.

Eyes glazed with boredom, Valentino eyed the slender blonde, uniformed in purple and gold. He signaled her to pour more wine—repeatedly. The more Valentino drank, the more Armand felt compelled to keep up with him. The wine, from a vineyard in Tuscany, was excellent. The entire dinner was exquisite beginning with marinated asparagus and prosciutto, topped by caper-stuffed anchovies.

"*Molto bene,*" Valentino whispered to Belle when the bubbling, creamy pasta was placed before him as the second course.

"*Grazie,*" Belle murmured, eyes dancing as she leaned closer to him across the table. When Valentino inhaled the aroma indulgently, George recognized it as the same sound he made when he smoked weed, overdone.

"Wait till you see the veal," Belle responded, eyes afire.

"Ah, sapphire fire," Armand mused aloud to no one in particular.

The thin woman in white silk on Armand's right glared at him. She continued eating, oblivious to him, but he remained silent, sullen.

Armand was startled from his daze by the sight of a perfectly pedicured foot in Valentino's lap, its thin diamond toe-ring sparkling like the chandelier above it. He must be hallucinating. He looked again to be sure Belle's foot was between Valentino's thighs. Both faces were composed, only a hint of arousal. A smile threatened the corners of Belle's mouth, her beautiful full red mouth.

Valentino's eyes, taking in Armand's reaction, smiled. A vision of the three of them together flashed behind Armand's eyes, but he was too stoned to see with clarity. Perhaps, Armand admitted to himself, not cosmopolitan enough for such an event. He looked hungrily from Belle's waist, up the lace-covered (just barely) breasts, into her eyes. Where he hoped to see a sexy smile of welcome like Valentino extended, he saw instead a look of triumph. When the navy blue eyes did not acknowledge him, the rejection set Armand off more than he would have believed possible.

He jabbed his fork into the steamy pasta and blurted, "This isn't authentic Italian cuisine. The pasta's mushy, overdone. Everything in this house is overdone. It's disgusting." He couldn't stop himself, but continued. "Chet, give us a tour upstairs. Show us around."

The woman in public relations at the opposite end of the table put her hand to her mouth, wiping away the forced smile. George exulted in making her eyes grow wider.

"Where'd you get funding for that gym, complete with hot tub, you installed?" he hissed. Chet's eyes popped open, bleary gray dots in the middle of yellowed marbles.

"Let's tell these guys from the Legislature tonight. How much, pal?"

The Legislator down the table, a short, heavy man with frog lips whose mind was keen, fed Chet a line, "I believe that remodeling was done with private funds, wasn't it, President Henderson?"

Chet's mouth fell open, his forehead wrinkled with confusion. He almost fumbled, but found the presence of mind to go the man one better. "Yes, indeed, a private donation from me. I installed the spa as a permanent contribution to the college. I believe this conversation provides ample proof of the need for a stress-buster for the president's family!" Smile frozen solid, Chet lifted his glass to a chorus of "Here, here."

Armand, somewhat sobered by the outburst, picked at the institutionally prepared pasta, which was actually quite tasty. When the conversation made its way back to the lull of academe, Valentino's sleepy eyes drooped, precariously close to his pasta. The guest of honor had not touched his food since Armand's proclamation though the others gulped it with the same forced enthusiasm they used to keep the conversation going and Armand quiet.

Suddenly a loud thud hit the table, shaking it. Valentino's face looked up questioningly from the plate of pasta where he'd buried his face. He peeled the cream sauce from his dark, bushy eyebrows—now striped caterpillars.

Belle took charge quickly, "Dahling," she said to the blonde server, "bring in the pinot noir for the next course but coffee only for Professor Armand. Make it stiff."

She turned to Valentino, a good-natured smile of indulgence softening the admiral's face that had flashed while she steered the table aright, "And now, you naughty lad, I'll help you freshen up." Her eyes twinkled with intention as Valentino allowed himself to be led away.

Armand inhaled the coffee, relieved that the husky voice in white silk made quiet, inane conversation until the guests were settled. Then the redhead apparently thought a suitable period of time had passed to make light of the situation. "Chet," she drawled, "What y'all got out in the slave quarters since you closed the guest house, a bondage parlor?" Even Chet chuckled softly as she leaned toward him, batting her lashes.

"Didn't we meet at a party in Georgetown after the inaugural ball last year?" the Legislator asked to distract her as the soft murmur of laughter following her question died down. Chet seemed a man at sea without the admiral until Belle returned, her mouth paler but puckered in a petulant smile.

"Valentino is exhausted. Jet lag is a demon. I assured him we'd wake him for the ball. A catnap can do wonders." The guests galloped through the tiramisu, ready to escape the tense combination of graciousness and denial.

Since the school was celebrating its 150th birthday, Belle had decided to throw a Sesquicentennial costume ball. Faculty arrived in outrageous costume, which Belle had anticipated: tweed blazers with tux pants and tux jackets with jeans. So immature. Several women wore antebellum gowns with hoop skirts, and a few of the older men dressed formally. Belle's waist was cinched so tight she never could've been "poured" into the dress if not for the merry widow, which pinched her flesh. She was afraid the garter snaps would give since her long legs stretched the elastic to the maximum.

Eyes surveying the crowd, Belle was astonished to feel a stirring—in spite of his ruining a dinner she'd spent weeks arranging—when she saw Armand. She hadn't noticed earlier that he was impeccably dressed in a navy suit, even a tie, his grey temples flowing back into the French-braided ponytail. He was incredibly good looking—his face like one of those beautiful Italian portraits staring from the walls of the Ufizi. He had such a flair for the dramatic, was considered outstanding as a teacher of theater. Her eyes feasted until she caught his glimpse, smoldered, then looked away. She could not resist toying with him.

Her lips curled wickedly when she saw him head toward her Ammunition Punch, which she'd begun to feel herself. Her plot for revenge began to take root as she watched him. She approached him at the bar, "May I have this dance?" she whispered, pressing her breast against his muscular arm.

He turned a startled face toward her, eyes limpid, then afire as he scanned her. The full, sensual lips pouted for a moment before he answered, "Why the hell not? Who could say no?"

Their chemistry, based more on hatred than love, was a force with its own determination. They rarely talked, had never really looked each other in the eye for more than a brief connection.

When Armand continued to dance through the third tune, she murmured into his ear, "I enjoy the satisfaction of dancing with a man who's taller than I am. At 5' 9, I was a wall flower as an adolescent."

"That's hard to imagine," his mouth mumbled against her neck as he pulled her closer. She pressed her breasts against the hard, solid chest and felt him stiffen in response. Belle relished the power.

"It's disgusting how many men won't dance these days," she sighed.

"Don't know what they're missing," Armand whispered, his voice thick from the evening's alcohol, then added, "You look hotter than hell."

"I usually am when I dance with you," she whispered. "And you look fabulous yourself, even a tie." She ran her finger along the smooth edge of the pink silk tie.

"Better not pull that out," he cautioned. "It might shock you."

"I can imagine," she purred, moving closer and playfully pulling on the tie.

"Take a look," he grinned. Belle glanced down, expecting to see some evidence of the stiffness she felt. Instead she saw, distinctly, a silk penis head in her hand. The lovely pink silk marbled into flesh tones as it neared the rounded tip. Mouth ajar, she realized the taupe designs at the knot were actually sketches of lush pubic hair. She struggled to maintain a poker face, then broke into laughter.

"You seductive devil," she smiled and moved in closer. They danced smoothly around the edge of the ballroom, Belle in the arms of a man she wished she could hate completely. Belle's impish face glowed under her short, silver hair swept into a small spike. Her gown accentuated the sleek, muscular arms she wrapped around Armand. He held her close, his warm breath against her neck. She closed her eyes, enjoying his firm lead, and let him momentarily take her away.

They danced farther and farther away from the crowd until she pulled him into a hallway whispering, "I want you now."

When she saw hesitation in the dark, smoldering eyes, she added, "We'll say we checked on Valentino."

In the shadowy hallway, he kissed her hungrily, hands all over her at once. She opened the elevator, only used for handicapped guests, unzipped his fly, and knelt before him. She pressed the intercom, which was attached to the emergency speaker that sounded throughout the campus. When she unbuttoned her dress, revealing the corset, his eyes devoured her. His mumbling was thick with liquor, "Mama mia!"

She disguised her voice, drawling a Tallulah-husky, "Signor Armand!"

"Is this love or something like it?" he muttered, hands squeezing her breasts around his penis. Her mouth found him. His breathing was hard, rapid. He was noisy, might as well have sung an aria. She snapped the intercom button and dressed quickly as an actress between scenes.

Belle let a dazed Armand out on the second floor and quickly returned to the ball amidst startled conversations about the origin of the strange noises: mouths gaping, hankies mopping, eyes bulging. She slipped into a group just before the startled hush fell over the crowd.

Belle managed to place herself in the center of the ballroom, her expression innocent as a virgin's, in time to see Armand re-enter the festivity from the plush stairway. His appearance at the head of the scarlet stairs interrupted the hatching rumors. Too far gone to realize why the silence had fallen, he staggered down the elegant staircase. Only moments later,

Valentino followed, scratching his sleepy eyes.

Armand and Valentino paused at the doorway, taking in the view of the city now that the fog had lifted. "Are these pecan trees?" Valentino asked, the word rhyming with the hand he used to point toward the thick umbrella of foliage that arched over the cobblestone road.

"We call them pecahns," Belle drawled, laughing softly.

"Charming. Perfectly charming," Valentino said, then handed her a monogrammed card. "My card?" he said, bowing formally. Belle tucked his card in her bosom, pulling the lace out far enough to reveal the edge of her dark nipple.

Slut, Armand thought, at the same time straining for another glimpse of the dark mystery of her nipple. He was too drunk to realize he'd been the butt of her joke, felt elated instead. He strutted like a celebrity. When she glanced at him briefly, Armand imagined her exclaiming, "Two points," as her long arms dunked a basketball. He was messed up, had to get straight before he went home.

Top down, hair blowing, the two men roared down the hill. Valentino lit the first joint, then initiated the singing this time, "Who's afraid of Virginia Woolf?" They sang to the top of their lungs, "La la lala lalah!"

Out

One of Rajena's colleagues said, as they donned their caps, "I saw your name listed in the wrong category, over there with the secretaries."

Rajena felt vulnerable, publicly exposed. The woman's enormous green eyes gaped at her under frizzy red hair, waiting for a response. Rajena muttered, "Oh?"

Rajena had been given the alleged honor of leading the procession at graduation, carrying the ceremonial mace. She figured nobody knew where she should march due to her recent status change. It was her last time to process since she was retiring, so they must have decided to let her have a thrill. Once on stage under the bright lights, she felt the thick warmth of the cap and gown. Her face flushed with the familiar sweat of menopause.

The commencement speaker told the graduates: "Three things you need for success in the business world are good morals, honesty and integrity. Inappropriate sexual activity will never get you ahead, mark my word."

A searing light flashed inside Rajena's head! She looked around the stage at the deans in their regalia—some of the most immoral, dishonest people she had ever known. Integrity was something the faculty talked about, but those who rose to power in the little microcosm where she'd spent her life usually had little integrity. It was a far more ruthless world than her husband's world as a pipe layer.

Rajena, giddy over the Freudian nature of the cold metallic mace she held, ran her finger along the rough, engraved *letters beneath her fingertips as if reading braille. For the first time, she detected the misspelling! Someone had misspelled* veritas *on the mace. It glistened under the lights: V A R I T A S, a shimmering, hot light radiating from it. Something snapped. Her feet took a mind of their own. She moved toward the president—the weak, hypocritical man who had inscribed the mace when he donated it.*

He had wronged her, and this symbol of the search for TRUTH—a word he couldn't even spell. The gleaming brass instrument was transformed into a weapon and she into a woman with a mission. She could see Jim's eyes widen, his frail body shrink back when he saw she was about to strike him. The gaping mouth was what she wanted, that source of deceit. As she raised the glistening mace overhead, she heard her own voice screaming, "OUT OUT...."

After that her lips moved, but she was unaware of what she said. Her arms raised the carefully polished mace and lowered it forcefully into the face of the frightened man— over and over. Blood spurted from his scalp, teeth flew, and his pale, thin arms fought the air around him as if he swam. Feet scampered underneath the flowing black gowns as the deans hurried off-stage. When the campus police finally restrained her, Rajena saw only the navy uniforms and the gleaming silver pistols in the leather holsters. Then everything went blank.

Rajena had taken seriously the charge of academia: to seek the truth. Always on the lookout at conferences for any shade of *the* truth (or any answers to her concerns for that matter), she made serious notes—grateful for what she learned at sessions her colleagues cut out on. "Sometimes at night while the others party, I grade two sets of papers," she told her husband.

Sammy Joe didn't believe her. "Um hm," he said from the newspaper.

She sighed, more frustrated when her husband erased her than when her colleagues teased her about being too serious. "I'm tired of sitting in my room alone, honey. You know you'd have a good time in New Orleans," she pleaded.

"Hell yeah, but not with those pricks. I can't stand being around that prissy Jim Wright. He looks like he's been rode hard and put up wet, and them lesbians you work with . . . hell, they just need a ridin', period. That's all the talking I'm doin' now, baby. Just drop it," Sammy Joe said, his face growing red.

"One of those so-called lesbians has a husband who's driving down on Friday—" she began.

He yelled so loud she jumped, "Drop it."

Rajena dropped it.

Maybe she started going out with the others because he didn't seem to care. Rajena wasn't sure why. She considered Jim Wright's invitations harmless enough. As Director of Career Counseling, he took a real interest in her position as advocate for learning-disabled students.

He talked a smooth line. "I just want to pump your brain, learn how to place the graduates you've worked with," he said, passing the steaming etouffée, when a group of them went to dinner at Toujac's, a quaint restaurant in New Orleans. "How do you like this family-style serving?"

"Nice," Rajena said, then added more wistfully than she wanted to announce, "Reminds me of home." She refused to think of Sammy Joe. He could be here himself if he'd chosen.

"I'm a family man myself," Wright said softly.

Rajena had heard otherwise, but she didn't give credence to rumors. Jim seemed sincere, sweet, though homely. Her room-mate tossed down a martini, and slurred, "Let's have a li'l fun, take in some jazz, go dancing after dinner."

The others quickly assented, but Rajena made excuses. Jim offered to walk her back to her hotel, "You don't need to be walk-ing Bourbon Street alone." He guided her through the narrow streets under iron balconies bulging with bougainvillea. The flo-ral scent and the night sounds were seductive—the wail of horns competing with soft, throaty laughter from the shadows. When they reached the lobby of The Maison Bourbon Hotel, Jim said, "It's early. Let's stop in the bar. Come on, Rajena, just one glass of wine. Loosen up. Besides, I have inside information about your new grant."

They talked mostly about work. He told her how ambitious their dean was, what the next ten years held for his division, how her grant fit into the plan, etc. Stimulated by conversation, Rajena became less reserved. The light drizzle outside had taken the poof out of her copper-colored hair, which fell around her almond-shaped green eyes like the shag cut students wore. Running her finger along the rim of her wine glass, she pointed to the lily in a slim crystal vase on their table. "What a gorgeous lily," she said, rubbing the petal.

His gray eyes lit up like a naked bulb as he whispered, "Tiger lily." Then he added in a husky voice, "Did you like the port?"

"It's delicious." She enjoyed the warm glow, the tingle it gave her. "I don't know much about wine, never tasted a drop until a year or so ago on one of these trips. I got tired of being the lone teetotaler."

"You're not a woman who should be alone in any way," he said. Rajena was astonished at the jolt of warmth she felt in response to the compliment.

Several months passed before the next meeting, a training session in Washington for all project directors. Jim, who had been promoted to assistant dean, managed to go to the capital city as often as possible. The first night, they were treated to a fabulous buffet at the Georgetown Conference Center.

Jim yelled politely as they tried to talk above the noisy crowd. Rajena recommended the smoked salmon remoulade and minia- ture crab cakes. "Nice wine, too," Rajena said.

Jim's mouth moved, but she couldn't hear his words. All voices were raised a decibel. The younger members of their group danced in a corner. "I can't hear you," Rajena shouted, bass drum throb- bing in her ear, "but I certainly wanted to congratulate you on your new appointment."

"What?" he yelled louder.

"Congratulations!" she screamed just as the music settled into a slow tune.

"Shall we?" he asked, formally. They danced stiffly, which made her feel dowdy, foolish.

"I'd love to hear your part of our conversation," he joked. "I have a bottle of port in my room, the finest made. Why don't we stop by there for a sip? I'd love to teach a bright woman like you about good wine. There's no bar here, and it's late to go out."

Rajena hesitated. She had promised herself a walk in Georgetown, which looked safe to her, but then it *was* Washington. "Sammy Joe warned me to be careful about going out," she said cautiously.

"Come on, you'll love it. I promise. It'll make this wine taste like Kool-Aid. Really."

Reluctantly, Rajena went, relieved to get away from the fevered pitch of the party. The wine was so sweet she couldn't believe it was alcohol or that it would relax her so quickly. Once she realized her thinking was as fuzzy as Jim's speech, she stood up, got her coat and sputtered, "Well, thanks, Jim. I'd better get back to my room."

"What's your rush?" His lips brushed her collar as she reached for her coat. "Maybe we could cozy up, watch some television," he whispered, flipping on a video he'd obviously planned. A redhead, with breasts astoundingly similar to her own, was taking a licking—all over—from a thin blond man with an enormous penis. Rajena was amazed at the titillation prickling her own nipples, now hard against the silk blouse. She covered herself with the coat she held.

Rajena had never felt physically attracted to Jim. He was so short, a slim pale man with a concave chest, yet the situation was attractive. She smiled at him, and suddenly he kissed her hard, moving far too quickly for her.

"Stop, Jim," she said as he began to squeeze her breasts.

"I've wanted you ever since I laid eyes on you," he said, gobbling her neck. "I know you've wanted me, too."

Actually, all she had wanted was someone to walk her back to her hotel, to dance with occasionally.

He was relentless, his mouth all over her face. "Jim, please, I don't want this to happen," she said.

"I do want it to happen, always have," he growled, forcing her to the bed. "I could help you with your career if you'd let me."

"No, Jim," she protested though a ripple of excitement struggled inside her, drawn to the danger of the moment, the exhilaration of the forbidden. Sammy Joe could kill this man without sweating. What was she thinking?

"Your eyes say yes," he claimed as he jerked at her pantyhose, ripping them.

"No, no," she whispered, now only half meaning it.

He uttered a hollow laugh. She closed her eyes as he disappeared between her thighs. She'd heard rumors that he and the librarian on campus had a huge porno collection. Jim was adept at foreplay, something Sammy Joe had never concerned himself with much. Head spinning after an intense orgasm, Rajena reached for Jim and closed her eyes as he unzipped his pants and, panting, plunged himself inside her. His strength was surprising as he pinned her underneath him, pressing her shoulders hard. When he was done, he passed out. She hadn't even realized he was drunk, which, furthermore, must mean that she was bombed, too.

She lay there: shocked, numb. She wondered if Jim had slipped some aphrodisiac into her wine. She had quit fighting so easily, lapsed into euphoria. How would she live with herself after this? She felt like a slut. Pitying hookers, she stuffed her feet into the uncomfortable high heels, which were too snug without pantyhose. At midnight she felt like a caricature of Cinderella's stepsister in the tight shoes as she retreated to her own room. She crammed the hose in the bottom of the trash can, filled the bathtub and tried for an hour to scrub him out of her.

Next morning when Jim acted as if nothing had happened, she avoided looking him in the eye. She didn't look anyone in the eye at the coffee hour, wandered miserably through the exhibits. She almost convinced herself it had been a nightmare. She decided to pretend it had never happened, too.

However, the next week Jim sent her tiger lilies at the office, a card jabbed into the center with the scrawled message: From your secret admirer. "Some secret," Rajena's secretary twinkled. Jim called her several times a week on some pretense. He never alluded to the incident, just pestered her.

In a month or so, the two of them were to attend a meeting at Hilton Head. Rajena hesitated, but decided to go ahead with the trip. She would be firm from the start, not allow herself to be alone with Jim.

On the plane, he pressed his arm against her breast as they talked. "Looking forward to the conference?" he leered.

"Yes, I've never been to an island before," Rajena said.

"Delicious," he said smugly.

"I have a headache right at the top of my ear," she answered, which brought a frown to his thin lips.

She asked the flight attendant, "May I move to those empty seats so that I can stretch out? I feel nauseated."

"Certainly," the pert attendant chirped.

Rajena exulted in the disappointment that covered Jim's face, his mouth sagging under the horn-rimmed glasses. "Feel better," he mumbled.

"I will," she assured him.

In the lobby of the airport, Jim rebuked her, "Since when did you get so cold?"

"Look, Jim," she said. "I don't want to spend time with you here, period. I'm sorry to disappoint you, but that night was a mistake. I'm not that way."

"I'm not ready for this to be over," he said, his face not an inch from hers. His wild eyes glistened with an eerie light.

Then she had an idea. "Sammy Joe is meeting me here. I think you'd better be prepared." She headed for the taxi stand.

He looked frightened. "You've told him?"

"Yes and he's furious, so you'd better keep your distance. I really mean it. Not just now but at home, too. He's dangerous."

"If you only knew what I went through to get the dean to send you on this trip," he whined.

She hailed a taxi and scooted in quickly, slamming the door. Her heart pounded so fast the raincoat that covered it trembled. Pulling the hood over her neat French twist, she told the driver,

"The Hyatt, please."

They only saw each other twice, both times in crowded rooms. She switched to an earlier flight and was home before he departed the island.

After that, he didn't overtly harass her. However, after he— inevitably—became dean, her career plummeted. No matter how hard she worked, she never moved ahead. It seemed as if every proposal she presented failed. She always met with *No* and worked down.

Ten years later, Sammy Joe still sat in his leather recliner, reading the newspaper or watching television as if he'd never moved.

Tall, blond and muscular, he was so good to look at that she had learned to live with his aloofness. His blue eyes were clear as a cloudless sky against the always-tanned face. It was hard to forgive him for having so little interest in her work until she looked into those eyes. Then it was hard not to forgive him. She never told her husband about Jim.

Rajena looked too buxom in sweaters by the time she reached her forties, so she covered her voluptuous figure with three- piece suits she learned about from dressing-for-success seminars Jim required. She concealed her cleavage, opting for high-collared silk blouses and bow ties. Sammy Joe teased her when she modeled her navy pinstripe suit, "Baby, folks'll be sayin' you look queer before you know it. I been wondering myself, 'specially now that you've made me watch those sex videos and do all that stuff you love." The look he gave her was an invitation, not a complaint.

"Sammy," she snapped, "you are so crude." She had begun to snap at him too often, but she got so tired, so frustrated. "I'm sorry," she added, "I'm irritated that I have to give up so much for this dissertation. I would've studied literature not studied those cloudy pictures of the brain. It's enough to make a sane woman crazy. They made me do this. Sometimes I don't care about anything any more."

He unwrapped a Payday candy bar and popped it in her mouth. She bit her half, salty peanuts stuck to the sticky sweet goo in the middle. "Chew on that," Sammy joked, but her creased forehead made him try harder to comfort her, "We both gonna benefit from it all though when you get that big fatass raise."

Once Rajena got her doctorate, however, the administration refused to give her the raise. Though they were practically strangers now, Rajena suspected Jim, recently appointed president of the college, was behind the sabotage. She decided to confront him.

Jim looked exultant when he greeted Rajena at the door of his office. "Long time, no see," he smirked. "Let me take your coat." Rajena could have sworn his lips brushed her neck. Strutting like a banty rooster, he led her to a corner of his office that resembled a living room. He waited until she was seated on the uncomfortable Early American sofa, then chose a chair that forced her to twist around uncomfortably to see him.

His decade-older, drab hair was thinner, had receded more, and his narrow shoulders looked mismatched with the protruding belly he'd acquired. He re-arranged himself, tugging at his crotch, then crossed his legs revealing his elevated boots. "You don't mind if I smoke, do you?" he asked, never looking at her or pausing for an answer. He lit the small cherry pipe, which looked like a toy, and tapped it. His balding scalp glistened in the harsh, fluorescent light.

He attempted to start with the normal pleasantries: small talk, mostly about himself. "I tell you, my dear, I have been so busy down in Montgomery trying to convince those niggardly legislators how desperately we need money here. You wouldn't believe how many hours I put in. Just the other night I told my wife—"

"Jim," Rajena interrupted, "I don't want to hear what you said the other night." She knew he hated to be called by his first name now that he'd ascended to royalty. "I just want to talk about my situation . . . now," she said, fixing him with an angry stare.

He was visibly shaken. "Well, then, let us dispense with formalities. We are expecting a freeze on all salaries due to proration. I'm cutting every corner I can."

Warped, twisted, he loved power games, and it showed as he crossed his arms. For him it was like hampering her tennis serve. Undaunted, she confronted him directly, "I would think you could make an exception since I'm working for a federal grant and my funding is different. I was guaranteed a raise when I completed my doctorate."

"Oh no, Dr. Kincaid, we cannot make exceptions; we must follow the rules," he said, unable to keep the grin from his face.

"I know you can bend the rules when you want to. Maybe I can't change your mind, but I can tell you what I think, which is more than I can say for most of the wimpy ass-kissers who come through these doors."

Rajena couldn't believe it was her voice or that she was exploding. She also couldn't believe how good it felt to let out the poison he'd injected into her. Eyes enlarged, he puffed so hard on the little pipe it looked as if he were sending up smoke signals.

Rajena continued, "Nobody knows as well as I do what meanness you are capable of. I refuse to let you rape me professionally."

Jim rose, swelled to his full height (which wasn't much), and said, "You don't have a leg to stand on with that accusation."

"My lawyer represented Wimp Sanderson's secretary. Think about it," Rajena snarled, snapping her attaché case. She had worn her highest heels to stand even taller than Jim. She loved the heavy ring of them as she marched out.

She rushed home after the confrontation, fixed herself a stout drink and went to bed in the middle of the day--something she had never done before. When Sammy Joe came in, he crawled in bed beside her and held her when she began to cry. She could have told him the whole truth then, but she didn't. She still thought she didn't have to. "You need a hot bath," he prescribed, starting the water in the marbled tub he'd recently installed. They soaked in the warmth for a long time, his arms wrapped protectively around her. Then they made love with a wildness, an abandon she had never known, as if he could reclaim her somehow.

"You can't let this stuff get to you, baby," he had said into her hair.

"I think I'm gonna see that counselor who helped your brother," she said.

"Good," Sammy Joe answered, dozing already.

Rajena withered when the counselor, icy blue eyes peering at her behind the oversized glasses, suggested, "You need to consider sobering up from workaholism even though those who exploit you pretend it's a virtue."

Slowly, Rajena came to her senses, began to take a second look at Sammy Joe and life after work. Still a handsome man in his mid-fifties, Sammy was sexier than ever. He had gone to see her counselor, too, a few times. Since then, their intimacy was much more intense. "Hell, I got $90 worth the first night," she overheard him tell his brother proudly.

Rajena brought less work home, took long lunch breaks, shaved hours off her calendar in the morning and late afternoon. She and Sammy Joe took a master gardener's class and worked hours in their yard, which had been neglected for years.

That's when her "affair" with Sammy Joe started. She often slipped off during the week to meet her own husband. On a gray winter day, she left the office at lunch, having listed committee meetings on her calendar for the rest of the day. She drove to the beach and still had time for a nap, a swim in the pool and a long, relaxing session in the sauna before Sammy Joe had laid enough pipe to call it a day. As she waited, hair turbaned with the white towel, she massaged her feet, slippery from the sauna sweat.

The next morning as the salmon sun crawled out of the ocean, they sipped coffee in the frigid wind. Rajena shivered in a thin gown and returned to the cozy room, telling Sammy Joe, "This must be what lovers feel. They think it's the person they are with— the unattainable married man—that makes them feel so good, but it's the escape from the ordinary routine and the forbidden thrill of breaking rules."

"Well, thanks, baby, you just made my day. I thought you had that glow because of me," Sammy Joe said, pulling on a suede boot. She grabbed the boot, pulled him back into bed, whispering, "Let me really make your day."

For years, she had noticed how her friends, if they were having an affair, could subtract ten years in an afternoon at a fancy spa. Now, she was enjoying the effects of pampering herself with body scrubs and herbal wraps. Meanwhile, because she had been so outspoken, Wright decided to punish her more—seemed, in fact, intent on driving her out of the arena altogether. The next spring when only faculty received raises, he changed her status from faculty/staff to staff even though she taught two classes in addition to administering her tutoring program. She simply rewrote her grant budget and gave herself a larger salary.

She had always insisted on teaching classes since that was what had drawn her to the profession in the first place. She loved the adrenaline, standing in front of a class at one of those moments when the students were enthralled. Their eyes would lock with hers, outside time, when they confronted truth in its raw form.

"Whose truth is this?" she asked them, always insisting they analyze the author's audience, purpose and tone. Finally, she taught long enough to convert herself: she began to alter her all-male syllabus.

She, for a while, enjoyed telling white lies to escape with Sammy. When he had assignments at Gulf Shores, Rajena could get up at five, walk on the beach, sit in the sauna, shower and be on the road by seven when Sammy Joe met his crew. She could be in her office by midmorning and feel the glow, the power of her secret, all day. Slowly, however, lying began to disturb her more and more. She hated being intentionally untruthful with her secretary who was so trusting; in fact, she began to hate all lies.

The morning after the fiasco at graduation, Rajena still heard a mantra running through her head. At first, she only heard the word *out*, but slowly the voice took shape. "I'm outta here, outta here, outta here," it said. The eerie voice was her own, but she wasn't moving her mouth.

She noted the unusually bright sunlight in the white, sterile room, the deep peace that had come over her. She looked at her watch; it was past ten o'clock. Unconcerned by the late hour of the morning or the fact that she was in a strange place, she closed her eyes and went back to sleep.

She woke up groggy in the afternoon, with a growing sense of apprehension. She had joked recently that when she took early retirement she would sleep for two years. However, she had never expected to actually do it, much less on the first day. Where was she? She slipped out of bed, went to the sink and washed her face with cold water. She blinked, then frowned at the swollen face in the mirror.

Her dark hair was tangled around her face, the red highlights picking up the sunlight—a few gray strands more orange. She smoothed her hair and tried not to notice the black eye with its purple rings. Her face was bloated from so much sleep, her mouth not as thin, the pleats above it filled in somewhat by the puffiness.

She raised the shade and squinted against the piercing sunlight as it flooded the stark room. She was relieved to see that she was not in a hospital but on campus with its familiar slope of land and the late-blooming azaleas bursting with color—red, pink, coral. Across the quad, the squat, brick administration building-- its slits of windows—told her that she was in the infirmary on campus. They had apparently drugged her overnight.

She opened the closet to find her clothes, but they were not there. Her hand at the throat of the faded hospital gown, she tried the door and found it locked. Rajena felt a cold sense of dread in the pit of her stomach. She picked up the buzzer on the bed and jabbed it hard.

She heard its shrill signal and then the voice of the nurse's helper, "This is Miz Dottie," she said sweetly. "How may I help you?"

"This is Dr. Kincaid," Rajena said, "I'd like to speak with the doctor in charge."

"Yes, m'am," Miz Dottie answered. "I'm afraid that little medical doctor won't be available until Monday morning, but Dean Anderson told me to call her at home as soon as you woke up. Soon as I call her I'll be in with a little something for you to eat. You just relax now, sugar."

"Yeah, right," Rajena hissed into the intercom. She dreaded dealing with the dean, a vacuous woman.

When the nurse padded in with a bowl of soup and a choco-late milk shake, Rajena laughed out loud. Miz Dottie looked like an oversized Betty Crocker with a wide, incongruous smile on her sagging face. Only an idiot could be so cheerful, Rajena thought.

"How did I wind up here?" Rajena tried to sound casual. She couldn't remember coming here. She remembered sitting on stage at graduation and feeling crazy, but she couldn't clearly order the events in her mind. She had felt crazy for months, but she had always remembered everything in order before.

"Honey, you shoulda seen yourself when they brought you in here. You had a bloody nose and a swole-up lip from fighting the police, all dressed up in that cap and gown, cussin' like a sailor. I told my husband, it just didn't go together, you know what I mean?" Dottie said, winking. Then she fished in her pocket and offered Rajena a piece of chewing gum. "Chew your troubles away?"

"No," Rajena said, both palms out in front to underscore the refusal.

"Now President Wright, he was a worse mess, I'm tellin' you," she continued. "They took him over to the doctor's office, had to take 12 stitches in his head. He couldn't say nothing. He just sat here with his mouth hanging open, his eyes popping out. My husband said it was prob'ly the most excitement the little feller's ever had. Lordeeeee, I'm tellin' you . . . well, I better hush my mouth before the boss gets here. Dean Anderson don't talk so openly with the patients, you know what I mean?"

Rajena decided Dottie might want to start a revolution of her own. Knowing she had made a friend with her act of rebellion, she convinced Dottie to find the clothes she'd worn under the cap and gown. When Dottie waddled in with the black slacks, Rajena winced to think she might get the dumpy little woman in trouble. "I promise I won't leave until I talk with the dean," she said softly.

Rajena sat up with a start when she heard the loud footsteps in the hallway. Dean Anderson, a tall, mannish woman with big feet, brought the loud footsteps inside. Sometimes Rajena called her Big Shoes to her back, laughing about the identical shoes of various colors. "She must order them from an Amazon Fashion Catalog," she had told Sammy Joe.

Dean Anderson was part of Wright's court of admirers. In reality she was one of his lackeys, often asked to do his dirty work like this morning. She wore a plaid skirt and a stiffly starched white blouse, carrying her navy blazer across her arm. She always looked as if she had on a school uniform.

"It's hot out there, this morning," she began in her incongruous little girl's voice, a smile covering her face. Rajena had served on committees with her at the church, had seen that smile which always signaled a showdown. Her blue eyes flickered with evil as she took a seat across from Rajena's bed.

Rajena was dressed now, but still sat in bed, propped so that she could see her magazine. She continued to flip through it, just to irritate the dean.

"How are we this morning?" Dean Anderson asked.

"Great," Rajena answered, continuing to read. Anderson was bucking for Vice President of Student Affairs, trying out her skill for handling difficult people, so Rajena thought she'd give her a challenge. The woman was a parody: huge, clumsy.

Dean Anderson cleared her throat and began, "President Wright has asked me to represent him in this matter. We feel you have brought disgrace to the university, and we want to keep the publicity to a minimum."

"I can sure as hell understand that," Rajena said, enjoying fixing the woman with a wild gaze. She cackled, making a witch-like sound deep in her throat. She loved the gaping, wide-eyed shock that replaced the dean's smiling mask. Rajena would use their claim that she was crazy to support her charges. The mental anguish had driven her to this.

"We can see that you are experiencing some serious problems. President Wright is willing to drop this whole thing since you are officially retired as of yesterday. We can put it behind us, if you will cooperate," she said, her sugary voice patronizing, maddening.

"That's mighty big of him," Rajena said, lapsing into the country voice she had denied for so long. She made her facial muscles twitch, enjoyed the puckered discomfort it brought to the other woman's face.

"Of course, we could press charges, you know. But we would prefer to stay out of court, play this down with the public. We don't want to create a stink, air dirty laundry in public." She smoothed the plaid-covered knee.

The shimmering light created a spotlight for Rajena to step

into. She cackled again and stood up, "You tell that pompous little S.O.B. one thing for me," she said. "Tell him to start readin' the newspaper real careful cause I know a reporter who is hot to have this story. My lawyer and I have a sexual harassment charge that will set this institution into turmoil for a decade. I'm not turning back now."

"But wait," Ms. Anderson said, her gnarled knuckles reaching toward Rajena.

Rajena was already beyond her, turning the door knob like the entrance to asylum. She wasn't sure how it would all come out, but she wouldn't stop the momentum if she could. "Y'all tell them whatever the hell you want to. I don't have a thing to lose, so I'm gonna tell the truth . . . about a lot of things!"

She let out the cackle again when she saw Dottie out of the corner of her eye, chewing gum and smiling. She kicked a trashcan clear down the hallway—its metallic clang echoing like ammunition.

MOVING

A ghost of myself in the window looked back under dark disheveled hair, the eyes puffy, dark underneath like a raccoon. I looked away; it was too early. We left just before dawn, the sky afire for half an hour. The mountains, in purple shadow, rose above the river as we approached the Appalachian foothills. The beauty was doubled by its reflection on the still water at Riverside—pale blue meeting the soft rose shades at the horizon. I thought of Easter eggs, then forced myself not to picture Mary Carson, my daughter. I blotted out the image of her father sprawled on the bed, reeking of booze and mineral spirits.

She was awakened in the night by his vomiting. After a coughing spasm he had strangled, then bolted to the toilet, spraying the waste of himself on the walls.

"Working on the mural again?" I mumbled sleepily when he returned with the perpetual wet cloth across his forehead. A stab of pity came close to penetrating the vomit-splattered wall between us in the bed.

Soon Mary Carson would be asking more than her innocent, "Is Daddy sick again?" I had to overcome inertia, make some choices. For her sake, I would.

Rob hadn't painted anything he'd been satisfied with for over a year. His teaching was really going to pot; I smiled at my word choice. My once dependable, fatherly husband decided he couldn't make art and teach, too. Now he just floated through the studio classes once or twice a week. The more

dope Rob smoked, the more he wanted to fight every admin-
istrator on campus. Increasingly paranoid, he thought the
dean was after him. I told him the dean should be. My gradu-
ate courses in counseling forced me to look at life realisti-
cally. I rarely noticed Rob's groupies any more, but Inga, his
latest "talented painter for an undergraduate" was harder
to ignore. He was downright maudlin last night, telling me
he's fallen in love. "Don't talk to me about love, Rob," I
snapped. "Solve your own problems. Don't bring me your dirty
dishes. Grow up, for God's sake!"

My icy voice had come from inside a glacier. I felt a sharp
pain at the top of my scalp. Otherwise, I had deadened my
senses, filled the ice tray of my heart so often it was frozen
over. I thought of Mama defrosting the refrigerator once the
ice was eight-inches thick around the freezer. I had prom-
ised myself a better life than Mama's, but now . . .

When I saw Inga scampering across the quad toward our
house before dawn as we drove out thirty minutes ago, I grew
another inch of frost in an instant. Thick chestnut hair blew
across her face, dangerously near the red glow of her cigarette. In the silver moonlight, her long legs glowed like phos-
phorescent tubes, the short skirt barely covering her panties
as usual. As the silhouette came closer, I recognized the floppy
hat I had discarded. Oblivious as usual, she hadn't even seen
us driving away. "Can't even wait 'til I get out of town," I muttered to myself.

"What, Mama?" Mary Carson yawned, pulling the small

suitcase behind her. She insisted on wearing her mouse cos-
tume from The Nutcracker *again this morning. The little grey*
ears shook toward me as she waited for my answer.

"Nothing, darling. Nothing. Won't Meemaw be tickled to
have a little mouse crawl in bed with her this morning?"

"She'll be scared. Meemaw's a worry wart," the mouse
squeaked.

I vowed that I wouldn't think of home again, turning back
to the sky that blazed now like a Constable or a Turner breaking out of its frame. I tried to focus on the conversation of my
colleagues.

I once resented these trips, my "professional responsibili-
ties." I looked forward to the outings now, viewed them as
rehearsals for leaving. I was surprised at the warmth crawling
over me like a sun ray at the prospect of being in Tad's com-
pany overnight. Things were always lighter, cleaner in his presence.

We hadn't traveled 20 miles before we started giggling. "I
have this friend . . ." I started. Georgia and Pat looked at each
other and laughed.

"What?" I asked. Tad looked straight ahead, negotiating early
morning traffic with the combination of recklessness and cau-
tion that men have at 25—mature enough to be responsible,
but young enough to have a heavy foot.

Georgia's full breasts were accentuated by the blouse she
wore, the hairs at the nape of her neck more carefully "care-
less" this morning. Lush auburn hair twisted and pinned loosely
at the crown, she looked great at 42 and knew it this morning.

She turned around to see if Pat was still amused. Then she explained, "Pat and I have noticed that whenever a student comes in with that line about the friend, it means they, themselves, have: a) come out of the closet, b) just lost their virginity or c) discovered they're pregnant and want somebody to talk to."

Tad laughed, his blue eyes crinkling. "I think I've tutored a few of those."

I protested, "Well, in this case it really is my friend because I was about to say that every time she has an affair, she loses 10 pounds. You can tell by looking that I'm gaining, not losing." I was conscious of my thickening through the middle ever since pregnancy. Georgia and I had both been pregnant at the same time, but her waist was smaller; otherwise we had the same body type. I tried not to mind that nobody reassured me my youthful figure was not disappearing.

Svelte, wide-eyed co-eds like Inga still admired Rob's broad shoulders and the soft brown eyes that first intrigued me. Though he was fifteen years older, I reminded him often of his beer belly, hoping to keep him humble and out of trouble. College students will sleep with anything that wears a mortarboard; art majors will sleep with plain anything. It sickened me to see the way their faces lit up when Rob smoked dope with them, still being naughty adolescents. Of course, it's even worse for a man in his forties to be so immature.

I enjoyed the distance from campus. It made it easier to

forget. It also made it easier to talk about things we'd been serious about at work all week. Georgia's tendency to play psychiatrist instead of teacher made me uneasy, but she did have more interesting anecdotes than the rest of us. Her dissertation was about some connection between sex and communication, which often led her off the path in my opinion, though I enjoyed the funny stories. "Tell Tad about the girl and the blow dry job," I said, remembering her latest fodder for howling.

Georgia shot me a look. Pat cleared her throat. "Oh come on," I said. "Tad will die! He'll love it." They thought Tad was straight-laced because he always wore a tie and a stiffly starched white shirt to staff meetings. He also had nice manners, an understanding of appropriate behavior. I knew his other side though, his lusty sense of humor. In the writing center, he wore L. L. Bean camp moccasins, khakis and a knit shirt open at the neck where the dark chest hairs peeped out provocatively, the same hairy glimpse at his sockless feet. He had nice skin, always tanned, and wonderful thick hair, which was clean and shiny.

I never would have thought I'd be drawn to a man so wholesome, so uncomplicated. The most attractive thing about him was his smile, the even white teeth gleaming under laughing aquamarine eyes.

Georgia began, "Yesterday I met with an overweight freshman just off the farm, for her weekly whining about sexual confusion. She'll probably never break away from 'mama 'n' 'em.' These kids decide they're gay when what's really happening is they feel loved and sexually gratified for the first time. This girl had an awkward fumbling experience with her lesbian roommate last month and she freaked over it, so I told her to try to find the same pleasure with her boyfriend. When I asked her how it was going this week, she broke into tears. She sobbed, 'I done what you told me, but then he made me give him a blow dry job.'"

Our giddy laughter bordered on hysteria. We had just enough sense to feel guilty for laughing about something we had no business knowing in the first place. "It's true. I swear to God," Georgia said, and we howled even more.

We offered varying silly opinions as to what could be done with a blow dryer, slipping into easy camaraderie immediately. We fell into that kind of trust that allows you—when you "retreat" from the work place—to reveal more than you would ordinarily. Tad and I told about the guy who tried repeatedly to write about *King Lear* when he couldn't read well enough to comprehend the plot. The boy had thrown us into hysteria when he said one day in frustration, "That Edward was a real bastard!" We were never sure exactly where he meant to go with that. The boy worked really hard, was very disciplined.

"He lifts weights every morning," Tad said, "and he probably puts that much into his studies but it just doesn't pay off."

I added, "The boy was so sweet, so diligent, that I cried several times after a session with him at first, but by the end Tad and I had to avoid looking at each other for fear of laughing about his bastard comment. Really. When he showed up at the end of a long afternoon, we either had to scream or cackle." I felt a stab of guilt for admitting the truth. The semester was over though and it was time for a break, so I gave in to the laughter, swapping stories all the way to Atlanta. In the city's heavy traffic, the beat-up university car swayed like a fishtail when Tad passed another car, keeping us cautious, team-driving.

Our musty, inexpensive hotel room, with faded carpet and peeling wallpaper, was at least clean. Georgia had said there was not enough money in her budget for Tad's room, so he'd have to pick up his own expenses. That arrangement didn't seem fair to me since he was the only one who wasn't being paid. He had worked hard all year for very little graduate credit but he didn't seem to care. Maybe money wasn't a problem for everybody.

After our meeting at Georgia State, we stocked up for the evening at a liquor store. When Tad saw that we were settled, he took the car and headed for some flea-trap motel he'd found for $15 a night. We indulged in girlish rituals, painting our toenails and trying out different hairstyles for the evening. Georgia said slyly, "I always do this when I travel. You never know what might develop."

She polished her nails with a deep red, cranberry polish. I used Pat's, which was a tamer red, more like watermelon. Bored by the girly stuff, I took a long nap. When Tad came back to pick us up, wearing a linen blazer and a paisley tie I was glad I had primped. We all looked our best, which lifted me out of the rut my life had become. Rob and I never dressed up any more.

After hitting several bars in Atlanta, we had a late dinner and came back to our room to continue serious drinking. Ms.

Georgia (by then, we were calling her by her plantation name—what "the help" had called her before she left her husband) said, "I take a nightcap to bed every night. Lots of times I don't even drink it, but I always want that last one before I go to sleep."

"Right," I thought. I knew she was a heavy drinker. I recognized all the signs.

I flashed on Rob, wondered how much he'd drink while I was out of town. He usually took that as an opportunity to tie one on. Mary Carson had looked so cute at Mom's, dragging the old leather suitcase behind her along with the mouse's tail.

I forced her image to disappear, gulping my drink. I was relieved to be indulging myself, not responsible for anybody's drinking but my own.

Pat took her shoes off and propped her pillows on the flimsy headboard. "Tad," she said seductively, "did you notice my toenails?"

"Not really," he answered, puzzled.

Georgia and I joined in, tickled, silly as hell. We took off our shoes and stood before him. "Come on now," I tousled his hair. "Let's have a contest. You pick the winner."

"They all look good," Tad said, his eyes traveling higher than the toes. "I'll take all thirty of them."

We had teased him all evening because we saw him eye the braless city girls. We even pointed out breasts, classifying them as melons or lemons.

After the toenail competition, Ms. Georgia decided to get comfortable, went into the bathroom and came out wearing a flesh-colored robe with floral print over a matching gown. It was soft, slightly sheer. Her skin looked smooth, silky, moist. I smelled the perfumed lotion as she passed—jasmine—a lovely scent. Except for her cow's neck, Georgia was a good-looking woman.

Tad tended bar, making each of us another bourbon and branch. He held his liquor well, learned it during the drinking rituals at Sewanee. He sat in the only chair in our room, talking and joking. I put on my gown, too, then crawled into bed, pulling the sheet around me as a robe. I hadn't expected to need one. The brown silk felt smooth against my calves.

When Pat started snoring, we decided to call it a night. I'd had so much to drink that I wasn't afraid to cross Georgia. I was angered again that she didn't split the travel budget equally. I said, "Tad, please don't get in that state car with booze under your belt. Stay here with us instead of going to that flea trap."

He looked tempted. Georgia enticed him, "Sure, why not, you could sleep on the floor. Look, this old carpet may be ugly but it's deep." She pushed her fingers into the piling, her breasts swaying as she stooped toward the carpet. "We could make you a pallet," she said.

"That's ridiculous when I have a whole bed to myself. You could sleep here, Tad," I offered, patting the mattress. I saw his hesitation and added timidly, "We could put some pillows between us."

"No," he said firmly. "I don't want to do that. Maybe the pallet's not a bad idea though. Let's have one more drink to help us decide."

"Just a short one," I said, feeling the liquor cloud my brain. I glimpsed the sad raccoon in the mirror, embarrassed by Tad's rejection of my offer. A little too drunk to deal with it, I focused hard on the conversation.

Georgia told Tad about her days at SUNY, the Southern belle bit I'd heard before. Gradually, I became aware that Georgia and Tad talked less and less to me and more to each other. In fact, there was an unmistakable chemistry. Suddenly uncomfortable, I wanted to hide or disappear, as Georgia's voice grew husky. Tad was leaning toward her, his drink sloshing, engrossed in her story. I pretended I was asleep like Pat.

"I sure would love to have a Brandy Alexander," Georgia whispered in a coquettish voice.

"Come on, then, let's go upstairs to the bar," Tad answered, "my treat."

"I don't know, I've already changed clothes."

"You could slip on that raincoat and come see what a $15 room looks like," Tad suggested.

Then there was no talking, but I could hear their breathing quicken. I never opened my eyes, but I knew he was kissing her. Then she cooed, "You really should go. I'll walk you to the door." He pushed her gently against the door and kissed her again, hard. I tried to pretend I was dead.

"Walk me to the elevator," he whispered. I heard the door shut as she went out in the hall in her nightie. I felt a swirl of emotion: titillated, perverted, envious. I liked feeling wicked. I never knew what happened outside, but after about fifteen minutes, I heard the ding of the elevator and Georgia's key opening the door.

"Oh, Jezebel," I exploded, giggles finally erupting. "You know I wasn't asleep." I felt energized by her high, the flicker in her amber eyes. Our uproar woke Pat up.

Even though I was loosened by the booze, I felt my throat tense when I confronted Georgia. I said it anyway, "If you'd shared the travel budget equally, you'd be having a lot more fun right now."

Her eyes flashed anger. For a second I saw that look she got when anyone crossed "the boss," but a smile replaced the anger and she laughed, "Yeah, all night long." We both laughed until tears came, a mixture of sorrow fading into the room as we cut off the lights and tried to sleep. I heard Georgia pour the nightcap, and then I closed my eyes. Done in. Tuckered out, melting into the peace of sleep.

The next morning I felt scratchy, confused, as I dragged my hungover body out of bed. I couldn't believe the energy the other two women had, didn't know if I could keep up with their pace. However, once I was dressed and through with breakfast, I felt almost normal. After browsing in shops downtown, we found a bar called The Midnight Sun. The name appealed to me, conjured up fantasies, but in reality it was just another place with a seductive name.

I watched Tad's eyes as they caressed every jiggle. I was magnetized by him, felt strange, like a voyeur. He and Georgia had acted like business-as-usual today. I didn't understand how, I had never even tried casual sex. I'm such an all-or-nothing-when-I-give-my-heart sort of person.

Tad helped me find a present for my daughter, a teddy bear.

Georgia and Pat were in another shop when he said it. "Shan-non, about last night ..." he began. My heart stopped. *He's not going to ask if I was really asleep.* He continued, "When you offered me a place to sleep, I hope I didn't offend you by say-ing *no*."

"No, of course not," I lied, blushing with the denial.

He openly admired my breasts, which sprang to life—hard against the low-cut blouse I'd chosen to accentuate them. "You have to understand," he said. "Maybe you're so sure of yourself that you can sleep in a bed with someone and feel nothing, but I couldn't. Certainly not with you. I mean, you're the most desirable woman I've ever known. If you weren't married to Rob, I'd be all over you."

He continued to look me right in the eye, his eyes so clear, not clouded with dishonesty. He was so direct I felt dizzy; I felt ten feet tall but also disappointed to know it was not gonna happen since I was married to Rob. I smiled, then hugged him. He had a teddy bear in his hand. I felt fresh and new and sweet when I told him, "Tad Larkin, you are superb. Think of all the heartache people get into because they want to hear that. Is your whole life that uncluttered?"

"No," he said, still gazing at me with those clean, clear eyes. His gaze told me it was more complex.

I felt a shiver, crossed my arms over the telltale breasts that knew what they wanted. "There's a lot going on with me right now," I whispered. "I don't need to complicate my life any further."

"I know," he said simply, then squeezed my hand. The warmth of his hand, its strength, jolted me. He looked away from the raw hurt that took over my face for an instant. Then we joined the others and continued to drink and shop until we found Emil's, a French restaurant Tad recommended.

The onion soup was sustenance to my soul as well as my body. I loved the smell of it, the bittersweet taste. Later, we went out to Lenox Square where Georgia and Pat shopped some more. Tad and I people-watched. I saw him watch the breasts: cones, melons, peaches . . . whatever. He looked at me playfully, "I'll be depressed tomorrow because my eyes aren't jiggling."

We laughed, then sat quietly—so comfortable, no need to talk. Finally, Georgia came up, laden with packages. "Why don't we head home before the afternoon traffic?"

"Great," Tad said, relieved, taking her packages. I saw them exchange a look. She liked being catered to, treated like a South-ern lady. He knew the steps of the dance.

I dropped back to walk with Pat. "I miss my little boy," she sighed. "Tad is such a nice guy, just like you said. He's managed to give three women the attention they need without any cat fighting."

We both laughed; then she continued, "He's so different from Buddy." A cloud came over Pat's plump, freckled face. "Sometimes I get so bored, so lonely for someone who talks instead of grunts." We laughed half-heartedly; then she admit-ted, "I dread going home."

"Yeah," I answered. That's as close as I could come to tell-ing her about my own dread. I never told anybody how miser-able Rob's drinking made me, how it raked over my emotional skin, bringing back years of pain and disappointment from my childhood. I stuffed that insight down as we climbed into the car, which was steamy after being closed in the sun all day. I put my head back and fell asleep by the second red light.

When I woke up, I felt fresh, rested, peaceful. Georgia dozed in the front seat, and Pat and Tad talked about her garden.

"Eating something right off the vine gives me a thrill, especially bringing in tomatoes and making fresh tomato juice; Buddy loves to make Bloody Marys with the juice."

"Sounds wonderful," Tad said his voice rich, flawless. "Have you ever made a peach daiquiri? You put the peaches in the blender first. When you put Chilton county peaches, dripping juice before you even slice them, in the blender, it's perfect."

"It sounds great," Pat responded without much enthusiasm. I felt flushed, responding sensually to the thought of warm peaches, tomatoes in the sun, their roundness like a baby's bottom.

I think of Rob, the warm, smooth skin, how close he used to hold me in the night. I remember the passionate eyes afire, slapping reds and blues on a canvas.

How could I compare a sweet, gentle boy like Tad who has so little experience, so little depth yet, to a man like Rob who has so much to offer the world. If Rob could only harness that creative flow again.

We were all quiet as we rode into Riverside at sunset— like weary cowboys at the end of a movie. Tad said, "This is the most beautiful time of day, but most people miss it, rushing around with dinner and struggling with kids who'd rather be outside."

The trees at the water's edge looked like dark lace against a woman's flesh, like the slip Pat bought. Maybe a splash of lace will wake old Buddy up, I thought. At least Rob does more than grunt.

Georgia stirred, waking up to see what loveliness she'd missed. She yawned, stretched, then lapsed into a jargon-filled warning to us about "re-entry."

Tad looked at the mirror's reflection of me. I turned my eyes heavenward, shook my head.

"Don't let your significant others make you feel guilty," Georgia continued with her warning. "They'll try because you have been somewhere getting your needs met. You automatically feel guilt because you thought you wanted to be home, but you feel a letdown when you get there, a disappointment. The kids pounce on the guilt like starving animals. I've experienced it so many times when I have a perfect getaway, a validation like this."

Georgia fingered the smooth silky band that made a V of her blouse. Tad smiled ruefully at her, and I knew in that moment whatever had passed between them was over. Back to reality for all of us.

I looked at the sky's fading colors, remembered the Easter-egg-morning sky. We were moving, but we were standing still, too.

photographer: Liz Hamilton

Loretta Cobb is director emerita of the Harbert Writing Center at the University of Montevallo. She has published short stories and poetry, but this is her first collection. She has written for the *Birmingham News* and is a freelance edtor. She is married to the writer William Cobb.